TELL ME TO GO

CHARLOTTE BYRD

BYRD BOOKS, LLC

Identifiers

- Tell Me to Go (Hardcover): 978-1-63225-055-1

- Tell Me to Go (Paperback): 978-1-63225-054-4

- Tell Me to Go (eBook): 978-1-63225-053-7

❀ Created with Vellum

His offer: 365 days and nights = $1 million

My addendum: I'm not doing *that*

His promise: Before the year is up, you'll beg for it

My days of lying and stealing are over, but then Nicholas Crawford makes me an offer I can't refuse. Spend a year pretending to be his significant other in exchange for $1 million dollars.

I tried to put that part of my life, and those hard-won skills, behind me. But I need the money. He needs a partner.

I told him that I'd never sleep with him. He promised me that I would end up begging for it. Now, I want him more than ever.

Especially when I run my fingers over his chiseled body and he **teases me** with his tongue.

Especially when he puts his hands on the small of my back and **kisses me.**

I want him so much I am going to scream. I want him so much...I might even beg.

"BEST AUTHOR YET! Charlotte has done it again! There is a reason she is an amazing author and she continues to prove it! I was definitely not disappointed in this series!!"

"LOVE!!! I loved this book and the whole series!!! I just wish it didn't have to end. I am definitely a fan for life!!! ★★★★★

"Extremely captivating, sexy, steamy, intriguing, and intense!" ★★★★★

"Addictive and impossible to put down."

"What a magnificent story from the 1st book through book 6 it never slowed down always surprising the reader in one way or the other. Nicholas and Olive's paths crossed in a most unorthodox way and that's how their story begins it's exhilarating with that nail biting suspense that keeps you riding on the edge the whole series. You'll love it!" ★★★★★

"What is Love Worth. This is a great epic ending to this series. Nicholas and Olive have a deep connection and the mystery surrounding the deaths of the people he is accused of murdering is to be read. Olive is one strong woman with deep convictions. The twists, angst, confusion is all put together to make this worthwhile read." ★★★★★

"Fast-paced romantic suspense filled with twists and turns, danger, betrayal, and so much more." ★★★★★

"Decadent, delicious, & dangerously addictive!" - Amazon Review ★★★★★

"Titillation so masterfully woven, no reader can resist its pull. A MUST-BUY!" - Bobbi Koe, Amazon Review ★★★★★

"Captivating!" - Crystal Jones, Amazon Review ★★★★★

"Sexy, secretive, pulsating chemistry..." - Mrs. K, Amazon Reviewer ★★★★★

"Charlotte Byrd is a brilliant writer. I've read loads and I've laughed and cried. She writes a balanced book with brilliant characters. Well done!" -Amazon Review ★★★★★

"Hot, steamy, and a great storyline." - Christine Reese ★★★★★

"My oh my....Charlotte has made me a fan for life." - JJ, Amazon Reviewer ★★★★★

"Wow. Just wow. Charlotte Byrd leaves me speechless and humble... It definitely kept me on the edge of my seat. Once you pick it up, you won't put it down." - Amazon Review ★★★★★

" Intrigue, lust, and great characters...what more could you ask for?!" - Dragonfly Lady

★★★★★

WANT TO BE THE FIRST TO KNOW ABOUT MY UPCOMING SALES, NEW RELEASES AND EXCLUSIVE GIVEAWAYS?

Sign up for my newsletter: https://www. subscribepage.com/byrdVIPList

Join my Facebook Group: https://www. facebook.com/groups/276340079439433/

Bonus Points: Follow me on BookBub and Goodreads!

ABOUT CHARLOTTE BYRD

Charlotte Byrd is the bestselling author of romantic suspense novels. She has sold over 1 Million books and has been translated into five languages.

She lives near Palm Springs, California with her husband, son, a toy Australian Shepherd and a Ragdoll cat. Charlotte is addicted to books and Netflix and she loves hot weather and crystal blue water.

Write her here:

charlotte@charlotte-byrd.com

Check out her books here:

www.charlotte-byrd.com

Connect with her here:

www.facebook.com/charlottebyrdbooks

www.instagram.com/charlottebyrdbooks

www.twitter.com/byrdauthor

Sign up for my newsletter: https://www.
subscribepage.com/byrdVIPList

Join my Facebook Group: https://www.
facebook.com/groups/276340079439433/

Bonus Points: Follow me on BookBub and
Goodreads!

 facebook.com/charlottebyrdbooks

 twitter.com/byrdauthor

 instagram.com/charlottebyrdbooks

 bookbub.com/profile/charlotte-byrd

ALSO BY CHARLOTTE BYRD

**All books are available at ALL major
retailers! If you can't find it, please email
me at charlotte@charlotte-byrd.com**

The Perfect Stranger Series
The Perfect Stranger
The Perfect Cover
The Perfect Lie
The Perfect Life
The Perfect Getaway

All the Lies Series
All the Lies
All the Secrets
All the Doubts

Tell me Series

Tell Me to Stop

Tell Me to Go

Tell Me to Stay

Tell Me to Run

Tell Me to Fight

Tell Me to Lie

Wedlocked Trilogy

Dangerous Engagement

Lethal Wedding

Fatal Wedding

Tangled Series

Tangled up in Ice

Tangled up in Pain

Tangled up in Lace

Tangled up in Hate

Tangled up in Love

Black Series

Black Edge

Black Rules

Black Bounds

Black Contract

Black Limit

Not into you Duet

Not into you

Still not into you

Lavish Trilogy

Lavish Lies

Lavish Betrayal

Lavish Obsession

Standalone Novels

Dressing Mr. Dalton

Debt

Offer

Unknown

1

WHEN WE ARRIVE...

I glance over at Nicholas Crawford as we ride the elevator to the penthouse of the Wailea Lani Resort and Spa.

He gives me a wink. He looks excited.

I'm consumed by terror.

Nicholas Crawford is an enigma. I don't know what he does for a living. I don't know how he makes his money. I don't know why he made me that offer. What I do know is that my desire for him is so strong it feels like an addiction.

The other thing that I know is that he likes to play games.

Not long ago, he sent me a check for almost one hundred and sixty-eight thousand dollars without leaving his name. It was only after I deposited it and paid off my student loans that he invited me to his home in Hawaii.

Then he made me an offer.

Spend a year with him, traveling, pretending to be his date, his girlfriend, whatever he needs, and in return he will pay me one million dollars. When I told him that there was no way I would ever sleep with him, he promised that before our time was up, I'd be begging him to do it.

His offer frightened me. But it wasn't because I didn't want to accept, it was because I did. Overwhelmed by feelings that I couldn't handle, I ran back home only to discover that my mother had made a mess of her life, only this time she'd put herself in real danger. The only thing that would save her was fifty-thousand dollars and Nicholas sent me the money without me even having to ask.

Why did I come back to Maui?

Sometimes, standing still isn't enough.

Sometimes, you have to take a chance.

Sometimes, doing something that scares the shit out of you is the only way to move forward.

I don't know if his offer is still available.

I don't know if I would accept it even if it were.

I don't know why we are pretending to be Mr. and Mrs. Landon.

What I do know is that when he touches my hand, he rouses every cell in my body.

What I do know is that when he intertwines his fingers with mine, I never want to let him go.

A woman with a long mane of curls comes up to us. "Thank you for coming," she says, shaking Nicholas' hand.

"Albert Landon. This is my wife, Olivia Thom...Landon," Nicholas says, correcting himself as if he had made a mistake using my maiden name instead of my married name.

The lies flow out so naturally, they feel like the truth.

Nicholas smiles at me, almost giggling, giving me a warm squeeze. We are supposed to be newlyweds staying at this resort for our honeymoon.

"It's a pleasure to meet you. Can I get you something to drink?"

"No, I think we'll walk around first," he says.

"Yes, of course. The bar is right over there."

Nicholas nods and pulls me toward the center of the room by my hand. Intimidated by all of the people in their cocktail attire and accurate life stories, I grab onto his arm and stay close to him. I want to ask him what we're doing here. I want to ask him who I'm supposed to be even though we already went over this.

A waiter walks around with glasses of white wine. Nicholas grabs one for himself and one for me. Now, we look like everyone else in the room. The penthouse is huge with various seating nooks arranged just so, giving the place an inviting feel.

I rest my glass on a tall cocktail table, but Nicholas nods for me to follow him. We smile as we walk past groups of people sitting on couches and around tables.

What mesmerizes me most is the view through the floor-to-ceiling windows of the wrap-around balcony, which looks over the ocean. Water goes all the way to the horizon and I yearn to be out there somewhere, instead of in this room.

"This is my wife, Olivia Landon," Nicholas introduces me to a group of people standing around a roulette table.

He thought it would be best that I use my real name so that I wouldn't forget to respond when he called me.

Nicholas purchases chips directly from the dealer and places six of them just on the outside line of two rows of three numbers. The point of roulette is to place the chips on the numbers you think that the ball will land on and this way he is betting on the whole block of six numbers. The dealer spins the wheel, releasing the ball. I watch the board and other people's bets. When my eyes return to his bet, all I know is that he lost some and won others.

"Oh, well." He shrugs and repeats the process.

"So, where are you two from?" the woman standing next to me says.

She has big hair and long nails and a thick nasally accent. She's also not playing and looks as bored as I feel.

"Boston," I say. "We're here on our honeymoon."

This is only partly a lie.

"Oh, how wonderful! I'm Kathy. My husband and I are celebrating our ten year anniversary. Second marriages for both."

"Congratulations," I say, shaking her hand.

"We're fellow East Coasters. We're from New Jersey."

"Oh, nice," I feign interest. "I used to vacation at the Jersey shore all the time as a kid."

"Really? Where?"

Shit.

I haven't practiced this.

I've never been to the state but I try to remember a city that I heard of from television.

"Cape May?" I say, but it comes out more like a question than an answer.

"Yes, of course! Great place. We're not too far from there."

I nod, letting out a sigh of relief.

"What do you do?" she asks.

"I'm an assessment writer."

Nicholas and I have practiced this. Just tell the truth, he said. You have an interesting job that you can talk about a lot and that's exactly what we need.

"Goodness, what does that mean?" she gasps.

I laugh.

"Basically, I write test questions for all of those standardized tests that kids have to take in schools."

"Wow, I had no idea that was a job."

"Somebody's gotta do it," I say with a shrug. "I write the math ones."

"Math?" She puts her hand over her mouth. Her whole body shudders. "I think I need another drink just to get over the PTSD that I still suffer from high school algebra."

I laugh. This reaction is nothing that I'm not used to.

Most people hate math and they aren't

afraid to tell me to my face.

"C'mon, let's let these guys play their game. Get a drink with me," she says, tugging at my arm.

My eyes search for Nicholas'.

I'm not sure what I'm supposed to do.

"Oh, get me some whiskey," he says, placing another bet. "You know what kind I like."

My blood runs cold.

Though I may know math, I know nothing about whiskey. Not even a name of a company that makes it. But Kathy waves at me again and I have no choice but to follow her.

2

WHEN HE TELLS ME THE TRUTH...

Kathy is talking my ear off as if we have known each other for ages. I walk up to the bar only half listening.

I'm not a very good liar and I do not think well on my feet.

My heart is pounding out of my chest.

I am cursing at myself for ever coming back here. To him.

"What's the best kind of whiskey that you have?" I ask.

"We have Johnny Walker Blue. Macallan Rare."

I've heard of the first one so I opt for the second.

"Great choice, ma'am."

"Wow, your husband has expensive taste," Kathy says, taking a glass of Pinot Grigio.

It feels like the moment when I should complain about something, so I roll my eyes and nod.

"I know, right?" I say. "He complains about how much I spend on my shoes, but then has no problem spending money on stuff like this. At least, after it's all said and done, I still have my shoes."

"My husband is the same way with cars."

We laugh as I deliver his drink back to the table.

"Thank you, honey," Nicholas says, reaching his hand out for the glass.

He takes a step toward me, bumping into Kathy.

She collides with me and the drink goes crashing down to the floor.

"Oh my God, I'm so sorry," I say, kneeling down over the mess.

Ice cubes mixed with glass and a puddle of whiskey are spreading over the wreckage.

I reach to pick up a piece, but the group of waiters push me away.

One of them carefully sweeps all the shards up with a little broom while the others blot away the liquid with a dishrag.

A moment later, it's as if nothing happened.

Nicholas helps me to my feet.

"You really didn't need to help," he whispers.

"I can't help it," I say, more for Kathy's benefit than my own. "I'm not used to having servers around."

She laughs and joins her husband around the roulette table.

"Well, it was nice to meet you, Paul," Nicholas says, tugging at my arm. "We'll have to get a round of golf in sometime."

"Yes, of course," Paul says without looking away from the table.

Nicholas gives me a small smile on our way out.

"What was the point of all that?" I ask, when we get back to our room.

Nicholas goes directly to his bag and

packs up the few things that we have scattered on the bed.

"We're not staying here?" I ask.

"No," he says.

I pack up my stuff and follow him to his car.

It is only after we drive out of the resort and disappear onto the highway that zigzags along the cliff that Nicholas opens his mouth.

"Thank you," he says without taking his eyes off the road.

"Thank you for what?"

He reaches into his pocket and pulls out a tennis bracelet.

There are six rows of diamonds with a delicate clasp in the back.

My forehead creases.

Where had I seen this before? Oh, yes, of course.

I shake my head.

Of course!

"But...that's Kathy's!" I gasp.

He smiles.

"What are you doing with Kathy's

bracelet?" I take it from him and examine how the high grade quality diamonds twinkle even in the faint light of the setting sun.

"This bracelet belongs to Theodore Grabinsky who bought it for his wife for their fortieth anniversary. She loved it dearly until her death seven years later from breast cancer. When Mr. Grabinsky decided to sell his home in Cincinnati and retire to his vacation home on Marco Island, he sold off his wine collection but kept most of his wife's jewelry, especially the pieces that she really loved."

Shaking my head, I try to figure what any of this has to do with the woman I met at the resort or why Nicholas lifted it off her.

"What does this have to do with Kathy?" I ask, raising my eyebrow.

"When Mr. Grabinsky went through his late wife's jewelry box," Nicholas continues without answering my question. "He was shocked to discover that this bracelet was no longer there. His property had not had a break in, not one that he knew about. So, he hired a private investigator to help him get it back."

A new song comes on through the car speakers. Nicholas skips it using the control panel on his steering wheel.

"Kathy Moreno's husband, Paul, is a dentist who spends his off hours running a pretty sizable bookie operation. One of his clients didn't have enough money to pay his debt so Paul accepted that bracelet in exchange and gifted it to Kathy on Mother's Day."

Nicholas taps his finger on the steering wheel and looks out in the distance.

"Of course, he couldn't tell her that the diamonds are all real and are of the highest quality because then he would have to explain how he could afford a piece of jewelry that costs more than a million dollars," Nicholas says.

"She doesn't know what he does?" I ask.

"Unfortunately, Kathy Moreno doesn't know much about her husband." He smiles mischievously.

I lean toward him eager to hear more.

"Paul's girlfriend is pregnant with their

second child and he is filing for divorce as soon as they get back home."

"But they are here celebrating their anniversary!" I point out.

"Paul got burned in his first divorce so he was smarter the second time around. He wants Kathy to think that the four thousand a month she will get as alimony in addition to keeping the house will make him suffer."

I shake my head.

"How do you know *all* of this?" I ask. "*Any* of this?"

3

WHEN HE MAKES ME CHOOSE...

"It's my job to know," Nicholas says.

I wait for him to elaborate, but he doesn't.

"So, why did you take her bracelet?"

"Mr. Grabinsky *hired* me to retrieve his bracelet for him."

I nod as if any of this makes any sense.

"This is what I do, Olive," Nicholas says. "A part of it anyway."

"How did ..."

"This is what I used to do," he interrupts me. "Back home, I developed a special set of skills ..."

"To steal?" I interrupt him.

"That's a crude way of putting it."

"How would you put it?"

"I learned how to separate people from their property without them noticing."

"Maybe not in the moment," I point out. "But Kathy will notice that she doesn't have her bracelet on when she gets back to her room. And her husband will know that it was the real one that went missing."

A speck of gold in Nicholas' eye twinkles.

He smiles out of the corner of his lips.

"This is a big deal, Nicholas. They may not know our names, but they saw our faces. The resort probably has cameras all over the place. We weren't in that room for longer than half an hour. We were the only ones who left."

My heart starts to beat a mile a minute.

I see the police knocking at my door.

They place handcuffs on my wrists.

They take me to the station, take my mugshot.

My boss sends me an email asking me not to come back. She doesn't care that my trial is pending. She doesn't care that I haven't been convicted of anything yet.

Two months later, my landlord sends me an eviction letter. I haven't paid the rent and I can't afford to do it anymore.

I have nowhere to go except my mother's place.

"How dare you bring me into this." I say. "I had no idea what you were doing. And I'm going to tell the police everything you told me. I'm not going down for this shit."

Nicholas' face remains expressionless.

"Can you hear me?" I ask, grabbing his arm. "Are you even listening to me? You have money, you'll be able to get out of this mess. But it's all going to land on me and I've worked way too hard to lose everything."

He can hear me, but he doesn't look like he's listening. I need to wake him up.

If he weren't driving, I'd smack him.

"Everything is going to be fine," he says.

"No, it's not. They're going to catch you."

"Kathy won't notice a thing because she still has a bracelet on her," Nicholas says slowly, savoring every word. "It's identical to the one that she thinks her husband gave her, dotted with Swarovski crystals and worth just under five hundred dollars. About the same amount of money that she thinks her husband spent on it."

I stare at him, trying to process what he just said.

"You switched her bracelets?" I ask.

"Yes, and you assisted by providing the opportunity."

"But how?" My mouth drops open.

I replay the events in my head.

I walk up to him with his drink.

Someone bumps into him.

He bumps into Kathy, who bumps into me.

The drink shatters onto the floor.

"You created the little bit of chaos that I needed to make the swap. It's all a game."

I scratch at the leather on the arm rest.

"Paul will only find out when he files for divorce and tries to take it from her. By then, he will assume that it was Kathy who is trying to pass Swarovski crystals off as real diamonds."

I nod.

"None of this will ever come back to me," Nicholas says. "Or you."

I can't resist the temptation to roll my eyes. That's what men like him always say.

They believe they are impervious.

They believe that nothing can touch them.

And maybe they're right.

Maybe nothing will happen to them because they're too powerful. But there are others, the ones that help them, who will lose.

Others like me.

"You don't trust me," Nicholas says. It comes out as a statement rather than a question.

"Am I so obvious?" I ask sarcastically.

I cross my arms and stare out of the window.

A bird flies in the sky somewhere in the distance. The jealousy that I feel toward her right now is difficult to describe.

Nicholas doesn't say a word.

Instead, he leaves me alone and lets me stew in my anger.

"You are not a stranger to this, Olive."

"Is that why I'm here?"

The road looks familiar now and I know that we're getting closer to his house. I'm regretting coming here again. I look down at my phone and wish that I had cell reception so that I could call Sydney.

"Sydney is staying at James's," Nicholas says, reading my mind. "You can call her when we get to my place."

"I'm not staying with you. This was a terrible mistake."

Nicholas turns down the music just a bit. "Do you want me to take you back to the airport?" he asks.

I take a deep breath.

Is that what I want? My thoughts all mash together, making it impossible to separate one from another.

"Yes, I do," I say.

A part of me expects him to beg me to stay, but he doesn't. Instead, he pulls over at the nearest turnaround and flips the signal that he's turning back.

"You're going to take me back now?" I gasp.

"That's what you said you wanted."

Our eyes meet.

I want him to plead for me to stay but his eyes remain cool and collected as before.

Not exactly dead, but completely free of expression.

The blinker makes a steady dinging sound.

As all other sounds disappear, it seems to get louder with each passing moment.

"Tell me to go," Nicholas says, motioning toward the road back.

My jaw clenches up.

My nail makes a deep indentation in the leather.

I don't want to go home, but I can't bring myself to say it.

He is so infuriating.

Anyone else would pressure me to make my decision quickly. They would urge me to hurry up already, but Nicholas has infinite patience.

Sitting back in the driver's seat, he stares straight ahead as the cars whiz by us in both directions.

"I'm really tired," I finally cave. "I don't want to go on another long flight."

"Does that mean you're staying?" he asks.

A dimple forms in the lower part of his cheek.

"Tonight, yes."

"Good." He steps on the gas.

4

WHEN I WAIT FOR MORE...

Y*ou're not a stranger to this.* That's
what Nicholas said to me in the car.
It was supposed to sound like a throwaway
line when in reality it was anything but
that.

I asked him if that's why I'm here but he
didn't answer. He changed the topic to
Sydney and he never went back to it.

But why?

How much does he know about me?

We don't speak the rest of the way to his
house. After parking the car, he shows me
to the same cottage I stayed in before.

"Where is everyone?" I ask, looking
around.

None of his staff are here now and the property feels almost deserted.

"They're off work for two more days."

I nod.

"We'll just have to fend for ourselves."

I nod again.

He smiles when he says that but it's a bit different from his other smiles.

There's a mischievousness in this one. A glint of hope, even.

I can feel his gaze on my body.

I know that he wants me.

I want him, too.

I've never felt this much desire for anyone before.

"Would you like to join me for a drink on the porch?" Nicholas says.

"Let me freshen up first and then I'll join you."

I use the bathroom and then look at myself in the mirror as I wash my hands. The woman looking back at me is tired but energized. There are few things in the world that are as exciting as taking something that doesn't belong to you. My only regret about today is that I wasn't in on the con.

I don't know how much Nicholas knows about me but he seems to be the type to do his research.

I am not here by accident and it is not just his affection for his dead sister that got him to reach out to me.

I knew there had to be something more to this. The thing that I didn't know was that anyone knew about my past.

"You used me," I say when he hands me a martini.

I stare at the slice of lemon that he placed on the edge and my mouth waters.

"Everyone uses everyone," he says, bringing his martini to his lips.

"Is this why you made me that offer?" I ask.

He stares out to the ocean. Somewhere around us, crickets and frogs start to sing their evening songs.

"What do you know about me?" I ask.

He turns slowly toward me. Glaring into my eyes he opens his mouth, pauses, and then says, "Enough."

"I doubt that." I shrug.

I'm acting smug but in fact, for all I know, he knows everything.

"Anyway, it's not a secret," I say, trying another angle.

"I doubt that." He smiles.

We drink our martinis in silence, unwilling to be the first one to speak up and show a sign of weakness.

"You used me," I start. "You told me the story but not the mark."

"You didn't need to know who I was after or why."

"It's best when everyone involved knows what's going on," I correct him.

"It may be preferred, but you handled yourself quite well going in on it blind," he says.

"You did that on purpose," I say.

It's less of a statement and more of an accusation.

"It was a test. I wanted to see how you would do under less than ideal circumstances."

"You had no right," I hiss.

Nicholas walks up to me, places his

index finger under my chin, and lifts it up in the air.

"I had every right to know what the people who work for me are capable of," he says stoically.

Of course, I think to myself. How could I be so stupid?

None of this is real.

He brought me here, told me a sob story about his sister, and made me think that we had some sort of sexual chemistry that we never really had.

That's the thing about confident men (and women), they *not* only lie, but they make you think that it's not a lie at all.

The best cons are those in which the mark, the person being taken for a ride, doesn't even know that they have been swindled.

Like Kathy Moreno. She didn't know that her bracelet was worth a million dollars and she didn't know that she'd lost a bracelet worth a million dollars. For the conman, it's a win-win.

"What do you want from me?" I ask.

"I need a partner. I have a number of

projects that need to be executed in the next few months. You are the best person for the job...or so I've heard," Nicholas says.

"From whom?" I ask.

"Does it matter?"

I lean on the railing and turn my body to face his. "Of course, it does. No one knows about my past. No one is supposed to, anyway. How do you?"

"Like I said before, I am very good at research." Nicholas inhales deeply, clearly agitated. "Now, if you're interested, I have one more test for you."

"I'm not," I say, narrowing my eyes. "My days of lying and cheating and stealing are over."

"My real offer is this. You travel with me, pretend to be my girlfriend, wife, ex, whatever I need for 365 days. In exchange, I'll pay you one million dollars for your services."

If he's offering me this much money then, not only must he really need me but these jobs must be bringing in a lot more than that.

"And forty percent of the take," I say.

He shakes his head, giving me a laugh.

When he focuses his eyes on mine, I show him exactly how serious I am.

"Ten," he says after a moment.

"Ten percent? Are you kidding me?"

"Don't flatter yourself. You're not the only pretty girl who can run a con out there," Nicholas says to deflate my ego.

But I know that it's just another bargaining tool.

"Thirty percent," I say after a beat.

There's a long pause.

I wait while he thinks.

"Fifteen," he says after a moment.

"Thirty," I insist.

Nicholas takes a step closer.

I can feel his breath on my skin.

His plump luscious lips are relaxed.

He opens his mouth a bit and I see his tongue.

A flash of heat rushes through my body. It takes an enormous amount of effort to keep myself from reaching over and kissing him.

He leans over and whispers, "Fifteen."

What a son-of-a-bitch.

"Twenty-five percent," I whisper, feeling my knees getting weak.

He takes his hand and runs it down my side.

A bolt of electricity rushes through me.

"Twenty-five percent and no sex," I say as sternly as possible once I catch my breath.

I state the no sex clause out loud more for my benefit than for his, as a reminder.

"Sex is not part of the deal. I already told you that you'll be begging me for it before our time is up," Nicholas says nonchalantly. "Fifteen percent. That's my final offer."

Angry with how the negotiation went, I give him a slight nod. He puts out his hand for me to shake.

"This handshake is contingent on how everything goes tomorrow night," Nicholas says.

"What's tomorrow night?" I ask.

"Your second test. One word of advice: leave your prudishness at the door."

5

WHEN I RECEIVE THE PRESENT...

After sleeping for fourteen hours straight, I wake up in a strange bed and try to remember exactly what I had agreed to the previous night. Things slowly come back to me.

The bracelet. The lies. The show.

A good con always requires a bit of a show.

It's not about brute force.

It's a sleight of hand.

It's about telling an outlandish story with a smile on your face or tears in your eyes, depending on what's required.

I stumbled upon this world by accident.

In high school, I spent my Friday

afternoons at the mall stealing fashion jewelry, makeup, and the occasional pair of jeans.

Then one day, a security guard at Marshall's stopped my friend Jamie Van Camp, took her to the back room and found that she had three unpaid for shirts on underneath her hoodie.

Back then, our modus operandi was to take a bunch of clothes into the changing room, put the ones we wanted to keep under our clothes, place a big pile on the clerk's table, and tell her that we are buying the rest.

If you were chatty and had a big enough mess of clothes, she rarely bothered to make sure that you had the same number of pieces to match the number with which we went into the dressing room with.

But one day it didn't work. The manager called the police and Jamie's parents, but her parents' lawyer convinced them not to press charges.

The following weekend, Jamie was ready to try her luck at Target but I was done with it.

If that had been me, I would've been arrested and my mother wouldn't have paid my bail so I would be stuck in jail until my hearing. No, I didn't have two caring parents who would save me from whatever mess I got myself into so I couldn't risk so much anymore.

I take a walk around Nicholas' estate. There is no one outside but the weather is marvelous and the crystal blue water of the pool calls to me. I slip into my bathing suit and dive in.

"One million dollars," I say when I reach the other side.

I spent all of my years in high school, and especially in college, working as hard as I could just to give myself a chance.

I wanted to get as far away as possible from the life that I grew up in.

I wanted more than anything to *not* be like my mother.

There is nothing wrong with government assistance and most people who receive it really do need it. But I knew that I could make my own way in life. I don't have any children and I wanted to make a career that I could be proud of.

I thought that after working for two years at a job that I would have some prospects.

I know that I'm due for a promotion to a position with more responsibility and maybe more money, but is this really what I want to do for the rest of my life? More responsibility and an extra thousand dollars a year still means writing assessment items all day long. And now that I have spent two years doing that, I don't have experience in another related field, meaning that I would have to start at the bottom at whatever new job I take.

I lie down flat on my back and float with my head half submerged in the water.

I have a good salary, that many people would give anything to have.

I have a nice apartment, a great roommate.

My student loans are all paid for.

So...why am I still considering this?

One million dollars plus fifteen percent of whatever our partnership brings in.

This is the kind of money that changes things. It's no longer just getting by. It's no longer living paycheck to paycheck waiting for your annual, one-week vacation.

This is the kind of money that makes a boss obsolete. If invested and allocated properly, this is the kind of money that could set me up for the rest of my life in a very comfortable life.

I fold my arms on the edge of the pool and rest my chin on top.

A tall white bird walks confidently among the lush landscaping outside of the wrap-around porch.

Given the prices in Maui, this house costs a lot more than one million but that million will go a long way toward getting me here.

I take a deep breath.

It's not just the monetary perks that make me yearn to say yes.

It's something else.

I have an itch that I haven't scratched since I gave up replacing sorority girls' Tiffany jewelry with knock-offs at Wellesley.

I walk back to my cottage to the sound of squeaking rubber as my flip-flops collide with the bottoms of my feet.

There was a time when an opportunity like this was all I ever wanted. But back then I didn't have much of a life.

To take this chance, I will have to give up my apartment and put my career on hold for a year.

And what happens if something goes wrong?

After taking a shower, I find a large box on the bed.

The note placed on the top reads:

BE READY BY 7. *Wear this.*

NC

THE BOX IS BEAUTIFUL, decorated in ornate swirls of turquoise and gold. I lift up the lid carefully and place it to one side. The contents are packed in perfectly folded tissue paper with a large gold sticker holding everything in place.

My hands shake as I try to peel it off, eventually giving up and just ripping through it.

When I see what's inside, I gasp.

6

WHEN HE SEES ME...

No wonder he told me not to be prudish, I say to myself, looking at the contents of the box. This isn't exactly something that a nun would wear.

I take the bra and panties that lay on the top. They are a matching set with the same light gothic design. They are both made from ultra-fine Bobbinet tulle and crisscrossing silk bindings.

The items are so beautiful, I can't stop myself from trying them on.

Looking at myself in the full length mirror, I admire the way the plunge underwire bra enhances the cleavage without the need for padding.

I run my fingers over the delicate tulle and lace motifs of the thong and linger over the gold rings and double elastic rouleaux sides.

Below another layer of tissue paper, I find the corset. It has a curved front hem with diamond-shaped paneling that wraps all the way around the back.

There's a knock on the door. A rush of adrenaline courses through my body. I look around for something to cover myself up with. The only thing big enough is the towel.

"It's not seven," I say.

"I thought you may need some help," Nicholas says.

Dressed in a two piece blue suit with a notched lapel and a three-button front, he looks me up and down with a smile.

"I'm not ready yet." I straighten my back.

"I'm not sure that's part of the outfit," he says, touching the welt pocket on the right side of his chest.

I adjust the towel to make sure it's tighter.

"Drop the towel," Nicholas says.

"No."

"This is part of the deal."

"What? You seeing me in provocative clothing?"

"No, you wearing *this* to tonight's event," Nicholas says. "All of it."

He motions to the corset.

I clench my jaw.

"This is part of the deal. The mark will be there and we both have to fit in."

I cross my arms and sit down on the edge of the bed.

"What's wrong?"

"I'm not going anywhere wearing that. I look like an escort."

"You're not an escort but this job may require you to look like one on occasion. So what?"

"So what? I don't need this," I say.

"Actually, I have a feeling that you do," he says boldly.

There's a rush that comes with doing something like this.

The anticipation alone is intoxicating.

It's like waiting for sex.

The foreplay that goes on and on...in some ways it's better than the orgasm.

But then, when you get away with it, a wave of relief sweeps over you consuming everything in sight...that's why I have to put on these clothes.

The anticipation starts to build. This is a costume that I need to be the person that the mark needs me to be.

I walk up to the mirror and let go of the towel.

Nicholas' eyes are on me.

They make their way up my body carefully but without a tinge of desire.

He is in work mode and he isn't looking at me like a woman wearing provocative lingerie.

He's looking at me the way that a designer looks at the set that he has just constructed. There's a window out there and a table to the left and a door leading backstage. All of the pieces are fake but the question is, do they look real enough for the audience to suspend their disbelief enough to get through the show?

Without another word, Nicholas hands me the corset.

It's a deep-cut, timeless, sexy piece made of Chantilly Leavers lace with satin panels and boning. The lining is made of tulle and it comes with four detachable suspender straps. He helps me fasten the hooks, trimming my waist and forming my body into the ideal female hourglass figure.

"Perfect," he says.

I glance at myself in the mirror.

Whatever insecurities I have about my body seem to vanish even though I am not wearing much when it comes to clothes.

Everything about the outfit is flattering and alluring. It draws the eye only to my best features while minimizing the rest.

"I don't have any pantyhose," I say.

"We'll just have to fix that," Nicholas says, getting down on one knee.

He gets so close to me I feel his slow deep breaths on my thigh.

Shivers run down my spine.

I shift my weight from one foot to another.

His fingers run up the side of my leg and tug at the first suspender strap.

It unfastens quickly, dropping into his hand. Instead of leaning over, he places one hand on my butt and another on my stomach and twists me slightly.

Another strap is off.

He twists me again, only this time his hand lingers a bit on my naked buttocks. I love the feel of my ass in his strong hands and revel in the moment.

He takes off another strap and unfortunately there aren't ten more.

I glance down at him.

Our eyes meet.

I can see his professionalism wavering.

I lift up his chin higher and sweep my fingertips across his lower lip.

My heart rate speeds up. He opens his mouth and wraps it around my finger, pulling it inside.

My knees get weak.

When they start to wobble, Nicholas grabs my butt cheeks again and spins me again.

"Two more straps to go," he says. "Stand up straight."

My legs feel weak as if I'm about to fall down. I take one step to the side and then another.

Instead of going up my side, this time, his hands hesitate just below the small of my back.

I clench my butt and then relax, allowing my cheeks to fall naturally into his cupped hands.

My body jerks and another strap comes off.

One last twist.

I adjust my stance so that he actually has to put some force into it.

He places one hand on top of the panty line and runs the other one down my butt, outlining the contours of each curve.

Fire starts to build within my core. His fingers run down the inside of my thighs and then back up.

He stops for a moment, touching the thong right between my legs for just a moment before continuing on and removing the last strap.

My body deflates from disappointment.

Nicholas smiles, pleased with his power, and gives me a little slap on my ass. "Let's go," he says.

7

WHEN IT'S TIME TO PLAY...

Luckily, the drive to this place isn't far because sitting in this corset makes it nearly impossible to breathe. The bones that keep the corset tight and in place, shaving inches off my normal waist and giving it an unattainably small diameter is the same thing that makes bending at the middle futile.

"How did you find out that I have a history with this kind of...work?" I ask.

I've never been arrested or convicted of anything before. I never told anyone, not even Sydney.

I always worked alone so telling others was an unnecessary risk.

By the time Sydney and I got to be close friends, I'd put that part of my life behind me.

I locked the secret up in a little box and promised myself never to open it again.

But that's the thing about secrets, if they are forced into a dark place, they find a way out.

"I already told you," Nicholas says. "I'm very good at research."

"But there is no one who knew anything about this."

"Just because there were no charges doesn't mean that there weren't people who had their suspicions about you."

My fingertips turn to ice.

"Who?" I ask in a whisper.

"It doesn't matter."

"It matters to me."

Nicholas shakes his head. "I do not reveal my sources. All I can say is that they're not after you. It was just a Tiffany necklace. She married a man who could buy her twenty of them a day."

I search my mind for names. The problem is that I had gone through so many dorm rooms and so many jewelry boxes that I couldn't possibly know every owner's name.

None of the women confronted me.

None of them even acted suspiciously around me.

"Why did you stop?" he asks as we pull up to a large manor house.

"I got close once. Close to getting caught. There was a big fraternity party that all the Kappa Kappa Kappa girls were obviously invited to. It wasn't going to be a lavish affair, more like the exact opposite. Raunchy and dirty with a mud wrestling pit for those who really wanted to impress the guys. None of the women were going to wear their expensive jewelry to this party and I had some time to break in and go through the merchandise carefully."

I've never told anyone this story before.

It feels good to share it now, especially with someone who understands the desire to take what's not yours.

The expert way that he lifted that bracelet off Kathy Moreno and replaced it almost simultaneously with a fake made me realize that he might be one of the few people in the world to know how I feel.

"What happened?" he asks.

"That night I got away with about ten thousand dollars' worth of stuff. I replaced them with good quality replicas that cost me about a grand, so that was a good night's work," I say. "But when I got home, something happened. No one suspected a thing and it had nothing to do with getting caught. I just felt...bad. I'd occasionally have these pangs of remorse over what I was doing, and they were debilitating."

Nicholas nods to keep me talking.

But I don't need any additional encouragement.

"One part of me would say that I wasn't doing anything wrong. It's not like these women deserved to get ripped off but they wouldn't even know that anything happened, so who was I really hurting? What was the big deal? But another part of me, the one that kept me up at night, would gnaw at my conscience. It doesn't matter if anyone knew what I was doing, it doesn't matter how much money they had or how little money I had, all that mattered was that stealing was wrong and I was better than that."

A valet opens the door for me and I step out in my sky high stilettos.

I am not an expert heel wearer by any stretch of the imagination, so I take each step with care and deliberation.

This way I don't look like I don't know what I'm doing, instead, I look like I'm just taking my time getting there.

"So, you haven't run a con since?" Nicholas asks, taking me by my arm.

I cinch my trench coat a little tighter around the waist and shake my head.

"I went to counseling to stop," I say. "But in order for it to work, I needed to divulge details, which I wasn't ready to talk about. So, I quit cold turkey."

He leads me up the steps and I lean on him for support.

"Is this something I should be worried about?"he asks as we walk inside a glamorous modern house with minimalist furniture.

A woman standing at a podium next to

the double doors at the entrance asks for our names.

"Thank you for coming, Mr. and Mrs. Puglisi, the coat check is right over there."

There is no one else in the foyer besides us and the thought of taking off my trench coat makes me sick to my stomach.

I cross my arms, tightening my hands around my shoulders to make sure that nothing can take my cover away from me.

But when we enter the adjacent room with a bartender and couples in various states of undress lounging, drinking, and laughing, my anxiety lessens.

The women are dressed in a lot more provocative clothing that I am and the men are hardly wearing anything except for tight underwear that leave very little to the imagination.

"Feel free to get a drink and explore the house. Different things happen in different rooms. This room over here is for socializing. Then when you want more privacy, you can go into the back rooms. Some are just for women. Some are just for men, others are for couples and another is for everyone to enjoy themselves together."

I hand over my trench coat and Nicholas takes off his suit jacket and loosens his tie.

Something comes over me and I reach over and unbutton his shirt.

He smiles.

"You getting in the mood?" he asks without stopping me.

I lick my lips.

It's not so much the others that get me excited, it's really just him.

Once his shirt falls open, I move the tie out of the way and run my fingers over each defined pectoral muscle.

They relax and flex with each breath and I bite my lower lip to hold back the excitement that starts to build in my core.

At the bar, I take my martini and watch Nicholas take a sip of his whiskey.

We make firm eye contact before he gazes down at my breasts. This very expensive bra does make them look amazing.

I glance around the room.

Nicholas' eyes aren't the only ones on me.

We are the newcomers here. Fresh meat. We're here to do a job, but first, it's time to play.

8

WHEN WE MEET THEM...

Carrying our drinks, we make our way toward the far end of the room where two groups of couples sit perched on a fat leather couch. The tall blonde has her hands on the crotch of the man next to her who is dressed in nothing but a black pair of James Bond style knickers.

I can see his massive package and she licks her lips as she feels it.

The couples are so engrossed in conversation that I wonder if they will make room for us.

They do.

The smaller brunette seizes her gaze on my bosom and immediately sits up and waves us over. Her legs part and cross at the ankles and I mimic her body position when I sit down.

Nicholas introduces us as Thomas and Meredith Puglisi.

Just a couple of everyday normal couples coming to a strange house to meet other normal couples they can hook up with. I can't help but smile at the ridiculousness of this situation. And yet... at the same time...maybe this is my chance.

As Nicholas talks and I nod and confirm whatever it is that he says, I turn my body slightly toward him and part my legs. The corset digs into my thighs but it also forces me to sit up straight and makes my breasts look fucking epic.

Danika Montezuma, the brunette, hangs on every word that Nicholas says while touching her face and lips. When he makes a joke, her skin flushes and she laughs nervously.

Suddenly, a pang of jealousy rushes through me like a bolt of lightning.

I am not Nicholas' girlfriend.

The only reason I'm here is to pretend to be his wife.

But this is not a place where regular rules of society apply. The whole point of this place is to break all rules of engagement.

Everyone here is either a couple or a single woman looking to get with someone else.

Some are into finding a third, some are into a full blown orgy.

So, if Danika wants Nicholas, there is nothing really that I can do to stop her from having him. Right?

I don't know.

I've never been anywhere like this.

So far it feels like a bar or a nightclub just with more scantily clad people. But the fact that if you like someone all you have to do is go to another room, makes it quite unlike any other nightclub I've ever been to.

"Meredith, right?" a beautiful man with messy cool blond hair says, putting his hand on my knee.

My cheeks flush and I flash him a quick

smile.

"Yes," I confirm. "What's your name again?"

"Jack Gilbert," he says, running his fingers up my thigh.

He lets his hand linger there, probably waiting for me to draw the line between what's okay and what's not.

But my eyes drift over to Nicholas and I see Danika's breasts brushing up to his arm.

He touches his jaw, and then reaches over to lift her chin.

I purse my lips, clenching my teeth.

Danika isn't the mark, and neither is Jack.

Why are we here wasting our time with them?

Why is he subjecting me to this?

Of course, the truth is that at this moment, I couldn't care less about the con. I'm again in the dark about most of it, expected to just play a part as his sidekick.

But watching him flirting with another woman, touching her...my jealousy tightens all of the muscles in my body.

My stomach hardens and my breaths become faster and coarser, getting lodged somewhere in the back of my throat on their way in and out.

Immediately my mind plays a game of comparison with my rival. I'm at least twenty pounds heavier. My thighs are much bigger. My hair isn't as shiny. My eyes aren't as beautiful.

But then she leans over to me and tucks a strand of hair behind my ear. Jack runs his hand on the inside of my thigh.

My eyes dart to Nicholas as I search his face not so much for help but for an explanation.

Instead of providing one, he just leans over and kisses my neck.

"Stay with it," he whispers.

I inhale loudly and lean back against the couch.

When Danika reaches for Jack, he brings his hands up to her face and kisses her.

They kiss each other by leaning across me.

For a moment, I lose myself in the way

Jack's toned body tenses and relaxes with each breath and then it occurs to me that it's okay to touch.

I reach over to him and press my fingertips to his skin.

He moans and I let them move down his body watching his mouth move around hers.

A quick jerk snaps me out of my trance.

It's Nicholas standing in front of me and pulling me up from the couch. Danika and Jack part long enough for me to get up before falling back into each other's arms.

"What are you doing?" I ask.

"We need to go somewhere else."

I follow him but reading the expression on his face, I can tell that this isn't planned.

No, it's not like something is happening or we are about to be found out.

It's something else altogether.

His movements are quick as if he is fueled by anger rather than a strong sense of purpose.

Then it hits me.

I stop in the hallway, pulling my hand away from his. "Are you jealous?" I ask.

9

WHEN I SEE HER...

"No, I'm not jealous," he snaps back at me. I smile. He's a good liar but not that good.

"Why are you smiling?"

I shrug. "Just find it funny."

"There is nothing funny about this," he says.

He leads me down a few stairs to another room. There are couples having drinks at the far end, but he pulls me into a semi-private booth near the entrance.

"I can't sit here," I say.

"You have to," he says. "I want to talk."

"I can't sit here because if I continue to

wear this corset for another minute, I'm
going to pass out."

As much as I love the way my waist
looks in this thing (this is the first time in a
long time that I haven't felt self-conscious
about my midsection), sitting in it is nearly
impossible.

"Let me take it off," he offers.

He spins me around toward the group
of four who were clothed only a few
minutes ago and are now almost entirely
nude.

As he unfastens one clasp at a time, I
watch as the women kiss while the men
open them wide and bury their heads in
between their thighs.

My hands get sweaty and I twist my
moon ring around my thumb in a circular
motion.

When Nicholas frees me of my binding,
he stands behind me and pushes the hair
off my shoulder.

Watching the man unclasping the
woman's bra, exposing her breasts while
Nicholas leans over and nibbles on my

earlobe, my body aches with the need to be touched.

"Tell me to stop," Nicholas whispers, pressing his mouth on my neck.

I throw my head back and expose my skin to his lips.

One of his hands makes its way down and cups one of my butt cheeks. My legs open wide on their own accord, welcoming him further. But instead, he tugs at my thong, pulling it up higher before letting it fall back in its natural position. The fire that started building deep within my core feels like it's going to explode any minute.

My hands search around behind me for something to hold onto.

It doesn't take long for me to find his throbbing dick and wrap my fingers around it. This is the first time I've touched it, and the size of it is quite impressive. I flip around to face him and reach down to unzip him.

While I fumble around with the top button of his pants, he pulls me closer and presses his mouth to mine.

When our lips touch, our tongues

immediately intertwine and I press my body as close to him as possible. This is the moment I've been waiting for.

I am no longer acting.

I am just using this as an excuse to do what I want.

My tongue searches for his and I bury my fingers in his hair.

He picks me up, spreads my legs, and wraps them tightly around his waist. His hands grab onto my butt cheeks and I feel his hard, throbbing dick pressing into my pelvic bone.

I want to rip off our clothes and push him deep inside of me.

I want to ride him and I want him to take me from behind, but all of those moves would require us to first separate and disentangle our bodies for just a moment, and that's completely impossible.

Still holding me tightly around him, pressing his mouth onto mine, Nicholas sits down.

He pulls his head away for a moment to kiss my neck again.

I open my eyes and watch as the

woman across the room climbs on top of the man who has been going down on her.

Watching her take him inside of her and feeling Nicholas' body underneath mine pushes me closer and closer to the edge.

A group of three people comes into the room, already with their hands all over each other's bodies.

The woman paws at the two men who position her in between them. She unbuckles one of the guy's pants and pulls him closer to her. When the other guy is taking his time behind her, she reaches back and inserts him inside.

My mouth waters watching her take what she wants from them.

She kisses the guy in front of her, first on the mouth then down his hard body. They crowd around her and that's exactly what she wants.

The one behind her slaps her butt just as the one in the front grabs at her exposed breasts.

Jealous of the attention that I'm giving

them, Nicholas tugs at my bra strap and pulls it down my arm.

My breast falls bare before him and he takes it into his mouth.

Finally, I look away from the threesome, tilting my head back consumed by my own pleasure.

When I look up again the girl is in the same position except that she's now facing me.

She looks familiar. I narrow my eyes to get a better look. It can't be her, can it?

"Sydney?" I whisper.

10

WHEN SHE SEES ME...

It takes Sydney a moment to process what she heard. I see her lift her head and look in my direction.

Her mouth falls open and she gets an incredulous stare in her eyes. The guy with his back toward me tries to pull her closer and that's what snaps her out of her daze.

"Olive?" she asks, getting up to her feet.

She doesn't rush but she does get dressed quickly. She grabs the silk robe from behind the sofa and cinches it tightly around her waist.

I climb off Nicholas' lap and take a few steps in her direction.

When she opens her arms, I reciprocate with a warm hug.

"*What* are you doing here?" she whispers into my ear.

"What are *you* doing here?" I ask.

Nicholas shakes hands with her two partners. It is only after we all take a seat around the table that I realize that one of them is James.

My eyes widen but I force myself to keep my surprise to myself.

A waitress comes around, hands each of us a menu of light refreshments.

The men quickly order a round of drinks while Sydney and I remain locked in our stare.

"C'mon," she says, tapping her fingers on my hand. "I have to go to the bathroom, why don't you come with me?"

I let out a sigh of relief.

Nicholas moves to let me out of the booth.

"You can't tell her anything about our job here," he whispers into my ear.

"I won't," I promise.

"You want a robe?" Sydney asks,

stopping at the table right by the stairs, pointing to the collection of neatly folded silk robes in both men's and women's styles and a variety of sizes.

Not having noticed them before, I'm thankful to have something to cover up my bare bum.

Instead of going to the ladies' room, Sydney leads me upstairs and out onto the wrap-around porch. There are a few people there, standing with drinks in their hands, so we take the path that goes into the garden for even more privacy.

"What the hell are you doing here?" We ask each other almost simultaneously and then break out in a gaggle of giggles.

We stare at each other and wonder who will be the first one to go.

"Have you ever been anywhere like this before?" I ask.

"Yes," Sydney caves. "A few times, in Boston."

"Really?" I gasp.

I sound like I'm judging her but I'm not.

I'm just surprised. We have been friends

for a long time and she has never said a word.

"I went to this club once that Tommy and Elise organized back in my freshman year. It was just in their apartment but basically you came with your boyfriend or alone and did anything you wanted with anyone you wanted," Sydney says.

"Tommy and Elise hosted sex parties?" I ask.

They met each other during orientation, a few days before the first day of classes, and have been inseparable ever since. They have two kids now and live in Connecticut.

"Some of the best ones." Sydney laughs. "They still do."

"Now?"

"They had this amazing one a month after they got back from their honeymoon when they closed on their house. It was pretty epic."

My mouth opens and I press my hand to my lips.

"Why haven't you ever told me this before?" I ask.

She shrugs. "You just never brought it up. And you were like the only person at Wellesley who didn't know about Tommy and Elise. They've slept with nearly everyone in our graduating class."

I shake my head and start to laugh.

"But I'm sorry that I didn't say anything. I should've told you. But I told my ex and he was not very happy."

"What do you mean?" I ask, tilting my head toward hers.

"One day, I sort of brought it up. Said how sexy I thought it was to watch other people have sex...you know, in porn...and I mentioned that I know about this one party. But he totally freaked out."

I give her a brief nod. Her ex was traditional and closed off and spent ninety percent of their time together belittling her and the rest pining for her.

"I kept a lot of things away from him, as you know, so this ended up just being another thing I put into a little box under lock and key," Sydney says.

"Your sexuality?"

"Yeah." She shrugs. "I just rationalized

it as I didn't need the parties. I could get what I needed from him. But that wasn't true."

"So, what happened after you broke it off?"

"The first thing I did was call Tommy and Elise." She laughs. "You remember that weekend trip I took to Vermont to pick apples and get some time to myself?"

I nod.

"Well, I went to Connecticut instead and went down on three guys while their girlfriends ate me out." She laughs. "Plus some."

"I was really concerned about you," I say, starting to laugh, too. "You were so fucking depressed. I wanted to go with you, but you wouldn't let me."

"Now, I wish you had," Sydney says, running her hand down the length of my arm.

"So...how did you end up here?" I ask, pulling my arm away from her.

"When I met James, I decided to be honest. I really connected and I didn't want to start out another relationship with this secret. So, I just came out and told him. And he was super into it!"

"Really?" I ask.

"Yeah, I was shocked, too. I mean, I thought he would get mad or just at least push me away. But he was really into going. He has never been but it sure didn't feel like it when we were in there."

"That's awesome," I say. "I'm really happy for you, Sydney."

She crosses her arms and looks at me. When I don't respond, she sticks her chin out and waits.

"What?" I ask, shrugging my shoulders pretending to be as innocent as possible.

"Your turn."

"What do you mean?" I look down at my hands and twist the ring around my thumb in a clockwise manner.

"Why the hell are *you* here? What's the story? I need all the details!"

11

WHEN I TELL HER PART OF THE TRUTH...

I bite the inside of my cheek. Glancing back at the porch I try to imagine what Nicholas would want me to say. I can't tell her about the con. I don't even know much about it but that part of the story must remain a secret.

"What's with the ten thousand yard stare?" she asks, grabbing my hand.

I look down at my shoes. With the weight of my body concentrating at the balls of my feet and my heels, pain starts to shoot up my legs. I shift from one foot to another, but it does very little to alleviate the agony.

"Olive, c'mon, you can tell me."

"Why didn't you pick me up from the airport?" I ask, buying myself more time to think. "You were supposed to get me."

"I know, but Nicholas asked me for a favor. You came all the way back here. I thought that you'd want to see him as well."

I rub the back of my neck and look down at the ground.

"What happened? Did he force you to come here?"

There's a real look of concern on her face.

"No, no, it's nothing like that," I say. "You're right, I...was interested. Am interested."

She nods.

"Can we sit down somewhere? I have to take these shoes off. My feet are killing me."

We look around the garden for a bench or a rock to sit on but it is all lush bushes and wild tropical flowers. There's a dew over the grass so it would make everything wet were we to sit down. Sydney tries to usher me back to the porch but I can't manage to take another step. Kneeling over, I slip off the heels and carefully place my bruised feet onto the cool wet lawn.

"Ahhh," I moan from pleasure. "Now, this is what I'm talking about."

Sydney follows my lead.

Neither of us says anything for a while and then she kicks at me with her bare foot.

She wants to hear the story and I have no choice but to tell her.

Not knowing exactly where to start, I start at the beginning.

I tell her about Nicholas surprising me at the airport and the way I felt when our hands happened to touch on the drive down.

I skirt over the forbidden details (how I helped *him* steal the diamond bracelet to get it back to his client). Instead, I bare my soul about the chemistry that I feel burning between us.

"So, how did you end up here?" she asks.

Ah, the sixty-four thousand dollar question. We're here for a job, playing a married couple who likes to experiment in the bedroom.

"He invited me here. It's part of the game...to make me really want him."

"Oh, really?" Sydney raises her eyebrows in excitement.

"Well, you know how he made that promise to me? That he wouldn't have sex with me unless I begged him?"

Her eyes twinkle as she nods.

"Bringing me here is part of that."

"Have you ever been to this kind of party before?"

I shake my head.

"How do you feel?"

"Well, I've seen them in porn but you know how it is, it's kind of like that but completely different, too."

"Yeah, I know what you mean," she agrees. "Real sex is a bit different from how it's portrayed on the internet."

"Anyway, he didn't tell me where we were going, but I had kind of an inkling about it since he did dress me up in this outfit," I say.

"Which is *exquisite!*" She enunciates every part of the word, savoring it in her mouth. "How did it all happen? I need details."

"I found the box on the bed in the cottage. He dropped it off while I was swimming. I wasn't sure what I was going to find in there but when I saw this...it was so beautiful, I had to try it on. I've never tried anything like this on before."

Sydney's eyes sparkle and her mouth opens in a wide grin.

"Then he walked in."

"What?" she gasps. I shrug as if that sort of thing happens all the time. "So, what did you do?"

"I let him help me with the corset."

"Ohhh!" she squeals, pointing her finger at me. "You...you're a bad girl!"

"It just sort of felt...right. I mean...okay, promise me that you won't tell James...

She nods.

"Say it out loud."

"I promise."

"Nicholas just makes me so...whenever I'm around him I feel like the ground is shifting under my feet. I never know what he's going to do next and that makes me want him so...much."

Every part of this sentence is true. I look down at my hands, which are trembling to the beat of my quickening heart rate.

"So, what happened when you got here?" Sydney asks.

"I think he brought me here not so much to be with anyone else but to seduce me," I say slowly. "We were watching people and it was so arousing. Then he started to touch me."

"How far do you think it would've gone if you hadn't seen me?" she asks, letting out a giggle.

"I don't know." I bite my lower lip. "I don't know if I wanted my first time with him to be here but at the same time, I wanted him so much that if he had stripped me and taken me right there, I would've let him."

My words come out quiet, almost in a whisper.

Telling Sydney the truth, however much of the truth I can reveal, feels like a burden is lifting off my shoulders.

The lightness in my chest and the fast pulse slow down and a wave of relief sweeps over me.

"I have only one thing to tell you," Sydney says with a mischievous glint in her eyes. "Nicholas Crawford is trouble."

12

WHEN WE MAKE PLANS...

When Sydney and I come back inside and find our men, I know that our plans for tonight are put on hold. I don't need Nicholas to tell me this, it's basic. Sydney and James know our real names and that means that we can't make contact with this other couple, or anyone else at the party, using assumed identities. There's too much risk.

"Does anyone want to come to my place for a night cap?" James asks and Nicholas is quick to agree.

Whatever was going to happen tonight will have to wait.

"That could've gone better," Nicholas points out.

By the way he was acting back there, it never occurred to me that he was that upset by the situation. I mean, yes, our plans have changed but we can just do this again some other time, right?

"What's going to happen now?" I ask.

"The mark flew in for this party, I'm not sure that he'll be in town much longer."

"This was the only night we could do it?"

He nods, clenching his jaw.

"What should we do?" I ask.

His eyes dart back and forth as he thinks. "We couldn't have done it with James and Sydney on the premises," he says.

"Obviously," I concur.

"James doesn't live far from here. Let's stay for a drink and then you can tell them that you're tired from the flight and we can come back."

I nod. I wouldn't say no to curling up in a warm bed right about now, but I also wouldn't say no to an excuse to run my fingers over his body once again.

James's house is much smaller than Nicholas' but very cozy and loved. He has traveled all around the world and displays his collection of souvenirs proudly. He has African masks from his trip to Kenya, baskets made by indigenous Mayan women from Guatemala, and an impressive collection of olive oil from his recent trip to Spain.

"I love to visit new places, but it's hard to fit into my schedule," James says, handing Nicholas a glass of whiskey.

"Being a pediatrician is pretty demanding work. Lots of hours," Sydney says proudly. They've only just met but she's already acting like a doting wife.

"I can imagine. Plus, flying out of Hawaii must add a ton of hours to the flights," I say.

"The long flights give me a chance to catch up on all the paperwork. Thank you WIFI, right?" James says with a shrug. "Hey, listen, let's do a toast."

We lift our glasses in the air.

"To the girls," he says. "Thank you both for coming all the way here and...into our lives."

Sydney and I exchange smiles while Nicholas says, "I'll drink to that," and clinks his glass with mine.

The conversation drifts from travel to what it's like to live in Hawaii full-time to what it's like to live in the Northeast. James is originally from Southern California, he got his medical degree from the University of California San Diego, and did his internship in Honolulu. He came here on a whim but stayed because he fell in love with the land and the sea. When he found a job at the main hospital in Maui he decided to stay for good.

"So, you'd never consider moving back to the mainland?" I ask.

"I'm not sure," he says, smiling at Sydney. "I don't really want to, but I guess I could be convinced."

Sydney reaches over and kisses him on the mouth. I haven't seen her this happy for a long time.

"On the other hand, Maui is much nicer

than Boston...so maybe my girl here can be encouraged to make the move instead."

"I'm thinking about it," she lies when we both know that she is almost as good as moved here already. "I have to find a job first and tell my roommate that I'm leaving her behind."

"Oh, is that right?" Nicholas asks, his eyebrows raising. "Is that what's going on?"

I look down at the floor but the smile at the corners of my lips betrays the truth.

"I thought that we had come to some sort of arrangement?" he whispers.

"What's that?" James asks.

Nicholas asked me to never tell anyone about the offer that he'd made. I didn't tell him yet but I did reveal it to Sydney. That was before I was planning on coming back.

I glance up at him and cross my arms to see what he is going to say.

"I asked Olive to come here to give me a chance," Nicholas explains. "Take a break from her work for a bit and just give... *us* a chance."

He pauses before he says the word us. Without revealing exactly what his intentions are to our friends, he has to come up with an alternative explanation.

"So, it's settled then?" James asks, lifting his glass in the air. "You girls are staying in Maui?"

Sydney and I exchange glances.

"We haven't exactly gotten that far yet," she says. "Nothing is decided."

"That's too bad," James says. "'Cause I'm not sure you'll be able to find two guys like us anywhere on the mainland. And you definitely won't find this scenery."

"Ask me again in a week," Sydney says, pressing her lips onto his cheek.

"A week is good. I'll take a week." He turns to face her and their mouths collide. Their desire for one another is contagious, making me reach over to take Nicholas' hand. He gives me a little squeeze before mouthing, *we have to go*.

13

WHEN WE DISCUSS TERMS...

J ust as I'm about to tell Sydney that we have to leave, Nicholas squeezes my hand and whispers, "It's off."

"What's wrong?" I ask.

He shakes his head. We can't talk now. A big part of me is relieved. I thought that I was looking forward to getting back to that house but running into Sydney and then coming here to relax has really altered the atmosphere of the whole event.

"Do you want to order some food?" James suggests and the three of us reply with a resounding yes.

"In that case, I'm going to have to change out of these clothes," I say. "Any chance you have something I could borrow here?"

Sydney shows me to the master bedroom, where half the closet is already filled with her clothes. Her suitcase is neatly put away underneath with James's shoes piled two rows high to accommodate the space.

"You don't waste much time," I joke, slipping on a comfortable pair of leggings and a loose pullover.

"Oh my God, this is heaven," I mumble, lying down on the bed and enjoying the feel of my body in something that doesn't poke and shape it in any particular way.

It's not that the outfit I wore didn't make me feel unbelievably sexy, it's more that I really hate wearing things like that. Letting the sleeves hang past my fingertips, I finally feel in my element.

"You look beautiful," Sydney says, tucking a strand of hair behind my ear.

"Earlier? Yeah, I felt pretty hot."

"Earlier...and now."

I give her a smile.

For a moment, I wonder if the fact that

we ran into each other in a place without many inhibitions is going to change our relationship.

But looking at the way she gazes at me now, I realize that nothing is different. We were best friends before and we are best friends now.

There is nothing romantic or even sexual about the way she is looking at me, she is just one friend telling another friend how beautiful she is.

"You looked pretty awesome, too," I say, watching her change into a pair of joggers and a crop top.

When we get back into the living room, the men are mildly surprised.

"What happened to the thongs?" James asks, making a dour face.

"If you are going to stuff yourself fully dressed, then so are we," Sydney announces.

The food arrives fifteen minutes later. While James and Sydney head to the front door to collect it, I turn to Nicholas to find out what happened.

"It's off. He left."

"Who?"

"Our mark."

"Yes, I know." I roll my eyes. "But you never told me who he was."

"He was someone who was there for two hours and who is now gone. Probably on his way back to New York."

Shit, I say to myself. I want to ask his name again but I hear Sydney's voice and I know that the timing is all wrong.

We don't hang around James's house long after we finish dinner. Everyone is tired and overly excited from the night's activities and Nicholas says that he has an early morning.

We drive back to his house in silence. I attempt to ask more about who we were supposed to do a job on this evening, but he doesn't give me much except for a few grunts. Since there is no radio signal out here, I go through his Spotify playlists to find something to listen to.

"All you have is Led Zeppelin and the Yardbirds."

"I have at least twenty playlists there," he corrects me.

"But they're all kind of the same."

"What do you mean?"

"Classic rock. Rock anthems. Contemporary Rock. Modern Rock. It's just rock, rock, rock," I whine.

"What do you want to listen to?"

"Something...soothing."

He grabs his phone away from me, scrolls down then up before landing on the Beatles' *Blackbird*.

"I was thinking something more folky but I guess that will have to do," I say.

"What did you think seeing Sydney there?" he asks after a moment.

"I don't know...I was pretty shocked. I never thought she'd be the type."

"And you?" Nicholas asks. "Did you ever think you'd ever go into a place like that?"

I shrug.

"Tell the truth."

"No."

"Would you if I had asked you?"

"You mean, if we were like...dating?"

He nods.

"I don't know. I really don't but..." My

voice trails off. I'm not sure if I am comfortable telling him this yet.

"But what?" He pushes me.

"Well, being there tonight...we were there for a job...but it didn't feel much like work. I mean...it was...really sexy."

I don't know why I feel so embarrassed admitting something like this.

It might be because I'm a woman and we are all told by society that having sexual urges is something that's wrong.

Or maybe it's just me.

My upbringing.

For men, sexuality and being aroused isn't limited to one person and no one blames them for that.

But for women? There's something wrong with it. There's something inappropriate even.

But if that were true, then who the hell are all of these men fucking?

"It is sexy," Nicholas says. "Watching you watch them...made me really hard."

His words bring me back to that moment, and I can't help but lick my lips.

"But the terms of the offer remain the same," Nicholas says.

"What's that?" I ask.

"If you want me to sleep with you, you're going to have to beg for it," he says.

"I accept your challenge," I say with a smile.

14

WHEN I GET A CALL...

The following morning, I wake up late, head straight to the pool, and swim a few laps before Nicholas shows up. As soon as I see him, I know he's agitated. His hands move around in little jerks as he asks about my night's sleep. He rubs the back of his neck as if he has something else on his mind.

"Are you okay?" I ask, giving up on making small talk. There's no point to it if the other person doesn't play along.

"I'm just upset with myself. With how everything went down last night."

I play with the ends of my hair.

It feels like I should apologize as well but I've done that already. I had no idea that Sydney and James would be there.

Neither of us did.

"Have you made your decision?" Nicholas asks, dragging his hands through his hair. "About my offer?"

"Did I pass last night's test?"

He considers that for a moment before giving me a small nod.

"One million dollars for staying with you for one year plus a percentage," I clarify.

"Yes, yes," he says quickly.

"How will you pay me? Every other week would be ideal," I joke.

"Done," he says, surprising me.

I take a deep breath and say, "I have to send my employer an official letter of resignation."

I expect a hug or at least a smile. Instead, Nicholas spins on his heels and starts to walk away.

"Send it today," he instructs before disappearing back inside the house.

Despite the chilly reception, I can't help

but feel giddy. One million dollars divided by twelve months is a little over $83,000 a month! That's more than I make a year at my old job. Divided by two, it's a payment of $41,667 every two weeks!

I dive under water and scream at the top of my lungs.

This isn't imaginary money. This isn't potential money that I will make if a con pays off. This is real money. He'll pay me this no matter what.

I get back to my cottage and open my laptop.

The words of my resignation letter flow out naturally and without much thought.

For a moment, I consider making it more formal. Then, I'm tempted to just write FUCK YOU.

Eventually, I settle in the middle and opt for not burning bridges.

The gist of it: *I am pursuing other opportunities.*

As soon as I press send, a wave of euphoria sweeps over me. My body feels lighter. My thoughts are clearer.

While I'm at my laptop, I check my email.

There are about fifty messages of promotional crap from various stores and companies I gave my email to. After I delete all that garbage, I remember that this isn't the only email account that I haven't checked.

The other one is through Corrlinks, a special email service that's reserved for communicating with federal inmates who are forbidden from using regular email accounts like Gmail and Yahoo.

I see that I have a message from *him* as soon as I log in.

Actually, there are three.

One written each day.

Owen and I have never been particularly close but over the last few years, our relationship has really blossomed. He went to prison not knowing how to read or write.

He struggled with reading since he was a kid. Mom always said he was just lazy, but in prison he learned that he was dyslexic. Luckily, the first penitentiary he was in had a program that prepared inmates for the General Education Development (GED) test. The teacher took an interest in him, helped him pass the test, and earn his high school diploma.

Owen learned quickly and now writes me long diatribes about the research he has done about the literacy rates among inmates (apparently, about 60% of prison inmates are functionally illiterate) and what can be done about it.

But that's not all we talk about.

We talk about my job.

We talk about his cellmate.

We talk about his plans for the future.

I usually write him three or four emails a week and fill them with enough detail to last him until my next message. He writes me one every day.

The first email continues the story of his cellmate's upbringing, the one he left off writing in his previous email. The second email tells me how much he's enjoying working in the kitchen and then concludes with a request to remember to write him again.

In his third email, he just writes:

OLIVE,

Where are you? Are you okay? Why aren't you writing me back? If you're mad at me, tell me, just please don't go dark. I'm your older brother and I'm worried about you.

Love,

Owen

I KNOW I can't *not* write him back again. But when I put my fingers to the keyboard, I don't know what to say. I don't even know where to begin.

I'M FINE. Don't worry about me.

I STARE AT THE WORDS. That's all I can really say without obfuscating the truth, but this is not nearly enough.

If this is all I send then he'll think something is wrong.

I never write back two sentence emails.

I never not explain.

I never not go into details.

I press my fingers to the keyboard and try again.

I MET SOMEONE. It's a long story but I'm actually in Hawaii right now visiting him. He's great, and fun, and amazing. Sydney insisted on coming with me since it's such a long trip. That's why I haven't written earlier. I'm sorry.

I READ OVER THE WORDS.

There is only one lie in it.

Great, fun, and amazing are not words that I would use to describe Nicholas.

A dark, dangerous enigma is much more appropriate. But how much of the story can I really tell him via email?

My phone rings.

It's a private number.

My fingers immediately start to tingle. I blink rapidly as I try to decide whether or not I should answer.

I press Accept.

I bring the phone to my ear. A robotic voice on the other line says, you have a call from the Massachusetts Correctional Institution.

15

WHEN A SECRET SLIPS OUT...

I bounce my foot on the ground as the operator tells me that I will be responsible for all charges. By the time I hear his voice, my hands are damp with sweat.

"Are you okay?" Owen asks, his voice is rushed and out of control.

"Yes, I'm perfectly fine," I say as calmly as possible. "I'm sorry I haven't replied. I was just writing you now."

He takes a deep breath. A sound of metal being dragged across the floor makes me cringe.

"What's going on?" he asks.

I touch my face and clear my throat.

"I met someone. We really hit it off and we've just been hanging out for a bit."

I'm not a very good liar, especially to people who are at all suspicious.

I'm not sure why this is the case given that I'm good at sleights of hand, shoplifting, and other tricky behavior.

Or maybe I'm just not very good at lying to *him*.

I tell him a little bit more about Nicholas, staying as close to the truth as possible. My voice changes in pitch and tone from nervousness but I hope that he attributes these changes to giddiness about my new relationship.

"So, how did you meet him?" Owen asks after a while.

My mouth becomes cotton.

"At a coffee shop near work."

I rub one hand with the other, noting how rough the skin is around my knuckles and how soft it is around my palm.

"So, what does he do?" he asks.

"What's with all of these questions?" I get on the defensive.

"I'm just curious. Because you never not stay in touch."

"Listen, I doubt that any of your cellmates in there have their sisters writing them every other day. So, I got distracted for a bit. So what?" I reply, defensively.

He doesn't say anything for a moment, and we both listen to the loud chatter going on around him. I can't make out any of the words, but there's yelling and agitation.

"Mom came to see me," he says.

Nausea shoots up my esophagus and I almost gag when I taste something on my tongue.

My hands become outright clammy.

Cold sweat drenches my underarms.

"She told me that you paid her debt to Marlo," Owen says. His tone is an odd combination, both accusatory and thankful.

"Where did you get fifty-thousand dollars, Olive?"

"Did she also tell you that she hired some idiot to shove a gun in my face so that I would turn the money over to him?" I demand to know. "Did she tell you that she tried to con me out of that money? That I had to track down Marlo on my own?"

There's a pause on the other end. Our mother, of course, never mentioned any of this.

Why would she?

In her mind, there is only one version of events - her version.

"She tried to steal the money from you?" Owen asks in a quiet whisper. "How did you find out?"

"I found Marlo and asked her. I wasn't sure how to do the exchange with that guy and make sure that he let Mom go so I thought I'd go over his head to the source."

"I can't believe that she would do that," Owen says. I clench my jaw. He has always had a soft spot for her. Maybe it's because the last time he ever saw her in the free world was almost ten years ago. Or maybe it's just nice to believe that your mother is a good person no matter what she does.

"Why did you still pay the money?" he asks.

That's the question I've been wrestling with ever since I got back. At first, it seemed so obvious but then...I started having doubts.

"Maybe I shouldn't have," I say slowly, "but I had the money and she still owed the debt. She had no way to pay it back. I wasn't sure what Marlo would do so I just paid it."

"That was a very nice thing to do," Owen says. "Thank you."

I shrug without saying a word. Tears well up in my eyes, but I push them away.

"Olive, are you there?" he asks.

"Yeah, sorry, yeah, whatever."

"So...I still don't get it...where did you get the money?" he asks.

"From this guy," I mumble.

"Wow, he must have some serious money," Owen says after a long pause. "What does he do?"

I shrug again but know that I have to answer.

"Finance," I mumble. "Real estate. He's got a few companies."

"He's not some old fart, is he? Some sixty-year-old taking advantage of you?"

I can't help but laugh.

"No, not at all. He's our age."

"So, his daddy must've set him up very nicely."

Owen's judgement makes me angry. Nicholas sent me fifty grand to help our deceitful mother out of yet another jam and here he is sitting in a penitentiary and judging him.

"He made every penny on his own," I say proudly. "Don't be such an asshole."

"Really?" Owen asks, his tone oozing in skepticism.

"He's also a local boy. From our neck of the woods."

"What do you mean?"

"He's from Boston."

I realize that I've made a mistake only *after* the name of the city escapes my lips. But it's too late. I can't force the words back into my mouth. I can't make Owen un-hear them.

Shit, shit, shit.

I want to scream at the top of my lungs.

16

WHEN HE TELLS ME A STORY...

"What the hell are you talking about?" Owen demands to know. "Your boyfriend is Nicholas Crawford from Charlestown?"

Earlier I had mentioned that his name was Nick Crawford but made it seem like he was just visiting Boston. It's a generic enough name to pass it off and Owen didn't question me. But now...FUCK!

I don't know what to say so I say nothing.

"Olive? Tell me you're not fucking Nicholas Crawford. *My* Nicholas Crawford."

"I am not fucking Nicholas Crawford," I

say. That part is true, at least. But his name used to be…"

"You don't know the first thing about him, Olive. He's a very, very dangerous man."

Goose bumps run up my arms.

"I used to run around with Nicky C, that's what he went by back then. We had the same boss but we had different associates."

"It's not the same person," I say, trying to make him stop.

But another part of me wants to hear everything that he has to say.

"Nicky C was ruthless. I've seen him execute a man point blank. That was something that pleased the boss and he rose through the ranks quickly."

I touch my calf muscle and feel it tighten with every word that I hear come out of Owen's mouth.

"Who was your boss?" I ask, wanting corroboration, proof, something that will tell me that he's telling the truth.

"You know I can't tell you that," Owen

snaps. "They listen and record everything that's being said."

I read between the lines. What he's really telling me is that *they* (the authorities) already know everything about this. Nothing he is telling me now is secret information.

"Eventually, Nicky C was in charge of all of the insurance scams," Owen continues.

"What does that mean?" I ask.

"A restaurant or a business doesn't pay their monthly fee once, twice, three times. The boss gets agitated. The only way he'll get back the money that's owed to him is through insurance. So, he sends in Nicky C and his crew to start a little fire. It can't have multiple points of ignition, otherwise it will be suspicious. Nicky was an expert in this. Whenever he started a fire, it was always small but powerful. It spread quickly. When the firefighters arrived, they took care of the rest."

"What do you mean?" I ask.

"They'd point their hoses and spray the whole place with water. They never try to preserve anything, just put out the fire. Most damage that's caused by fires comes from water. Whenever Nicky C started a fire, the insurance company always paid out."

I lean back in the chair and take it all in.

What are the chances that he's talking about someone else?

What if he's wrong?

"I don't think it's the same person," I say after a moment.

"Nicky C vanished one day after his partner showed up dead," Owen says, ignoring me. "The boss thought that he just decided to take some time off, maybe went down to Florida for some rest and relaxation. But days turned into weeks and Nicky didn't come back."

"This isn't the same guy," I insist.

"It took a few months before we all figured out what happened. The two of them had a side job of breaking into wealthy homes out there in the country while the owners were away in Martha's Vineyard or wherever the fuck they went. At first, it was a few pieces of jewelry, some antiques but then their hauls got bigger and bigger."

I put my hand on my chest and listen to the way my breath bursts in and out.

"To say that they were good would be an understatement. They broke into secure homes with guards. They broke into safes. After casing the joint, the job took two trips. The first they would photograph and measure everything they found so that they could make replicas and, on the second, they would return for the pieces and make the switch."

"How do you know any of this?"

"They found the guy who made the replicas," Owen says.

"The police?"

He laughs. "No, our boss."

My body starts to rock from side to side. I don't want to believe this but I can't ignore the truth. His approach hasn't changed much. I've seen it in action. I was an integral part of it.

"The replicas were an integral part of the plan," Owen explains even though he doesn't have to. "Without them, the owners would know immediately that the jewelry was missing. They'd call the police. They'd hire a private investigator. But with the replicas, months would pass before anyone noticed. The jewelry was just as heavy. It looked the same. The only thing that was different was that it wasn't made of real diamonds."

I curl my shoulders forward, caving my chest in.

This can't be true.

This can't be my Nicholas.

"My boss has been looking for him ever since he disappeared. The rule was that you were supposed to hand over seventy percent of whatever you took in on the side, since side jobs weren't exactly legal. Neither Nicky C nor his partner ever gave him a cent."

"Well, they were their hauls," I say quietly.

"The last thing that the replica guy made was a Harry Winston necklace worth over two million dollars. The night that they broke into that estate on Nantucket to make the exchange, they found his partner's body in the Belle Isle Marsh."

"I don't know why you're telling me all of this."

"Because you're with him and he's a dangerous man. He killed two people that I know of and who knows how many others," Owen says.

"It's not him," I say under my breath. "Crawford isn't even his real name."

Without missing a beat, Owen says, "He used to use his biological father's real name, Reed. But when he was in high school, he changed it."

I rub the back of my neck. I'm drowning under the flow of information unable to come up for air.

"You don't know if it's the same person," I insist. "Nicholas Crawford is a generic name. Besides, why the hell would he still use that name if everyone knew it?"

"Everyone knew him as Nicky C. Besides, he was always cocky, and an arrogant enough bastard to keep his old name. As a fuck you to the boss, to his associates, to me."

"You?" I ask.

"I've had some...dealings with him myself. We didn't exactly leave on the best of terms."

"What happened?" I ask.

There's a long pause.

"You know I can't talk about any of that here. I'm due for a parole hearing soon. I can't implicate myself in anything. But it was nothing illegal."

I furrow my brow until I realize that he had added that last sentence for the recording. His previous statement was a sidestep, it wasn't anything that he should've said.

"You need to stay away from him, Olive. You need to just ghost him until he stops calling. He probably doesn't know that I'm your brother. You did just meet in the coffee shop, right? Just ghost him for a while until he gets the point. He has a short attention span when it comes to females."

I clench my jaw. I've always hated the way some men refer to women as females. The word is so scientific and cold.

"I can't do that," I say quietly.

"Why not? Because you have *feelings* for him?" he says in a mocking fashion. When I don't reply, something occurs to him.

"Oh, shit, I forgot. You took fifty grand from him. Fuck!"

"What are you talking about?" I ask.

"You took Mom's debt from Marlo and now you owe Nicky C a debt. That's...that's *not* good, Olive."

I hear a tinge of fear, something that I'm not used to hearing from Owen.

"I don't owe any debt to Nicholas Crawford or this Nicky C," I explain. "He doesn't even know the details of why I needed the money."

A robotic voice interrupts our conversation. "You have one minute remaining."

"Get the fuck out of the city, Olive!" Owen says. "Drive, drive out west. Buy some new documents. Start a new life. Run as far as you can!"

17

WHEN HE ASKS ME FOR A FAVOR...

Owen's words reverberate in my head long after he hangs up. It's exactly the advice that I gave our mom when I heard about her debt. I cradle my phone in my lap and run my fingers around its soft corners.

His words come back to haunt me. I try to convince myself that he's lying. No, not lying, wrong.

Nicky C is not Nicholas Crawford.

It's a common name and he wouldn't be stupid enough to use it if he were trying to live under a different identity.

But that's a big if.

My attempts to convince myself fall flat.

Nicholas Crawford is Ashley's brother. We all grew up in the same neighborhood and city.

He told me that the reason he wasn't there for her was that he was running the streets.

That's a euphemism for being in a gang, or part of some sort of organized crime syndicate.

He didn't try to hide it. In that case, chances are he knew Owen, or at least of him.

Does that mean that he wanted me to tell Owen? Does that mean that he didn't care if he were found out?

Besides these and about a million other questions, there is the undeniable truth. Nicky C worked with replicas and only stole things that he could replace with these fake trinkets. That's exactly what Nicholas Crawford did to get Kathy Moreno's bracelet.

But what about that story he told me? It came out so naturally. So effervescently. Like he didn't have to think about it once. As if it was the whole truth and nothing but the truth.

That's what people like us do, though, isn't it? We lie.

We cheat.

We deceive.

So, why *wouldn't* he lie to me?

My phone rings again. My body jolts from surprise. It's another collect call. Owen got more time.

"What are you going to do?" he asks, his words dripping with fear.

"I don't know. I'm sitting here trying to figure it out."

"You need to run, Olive."

"I can't."

"You need to get out of Boston."

"I can't."

"Why not?"

"I'm not there," I say quietly. "I'm in...Hawaii."

"What?" he snaps.

"Maui, to be exact."

He takes a deep breath. "Why the fuck are you in Maui?"

"Nicholas invited me. We're here on vacation."

"Fuck, fuck, fuck," Owen whispers under his breath.

"Listen, I'm fine. You don't have to worry about me. Nicholas is...a really great guy. He has this amazing house here and we are really getting along."

"You are so stupid, Olive," Owen says. "How can you be so smart and such an idiot at the same time?"

I purse my lips. Anger starts to rise from the pit of my stomach.

"Please don't put me down, okay? I get enough of that from Mom."

"I'm sorry. I shouldn't have said that." His tone changes immediately. "I am just so worried about you."

"I'm going to be fine."

"You keep saying that but it's not going to make it anymore true. How about this? How about you just say you have to get back home for something and come back to Boston?"

"I thought you told me to get away from Boston?"

"That's when I thought that's where you both were. But I should've known that he was a coward who was going to be hiding out in some billionaire's paradise while the rest of us rot in prison."

This jealously gives me pause for concern.

"What did he do to you exactly?"

This catches Owen by surprise. He clears his throat and then mumbles, "No, nothing. He didn't do anything to me...but the organization suffered and he killed his partner..."

I narrow my eyes and press the phone closer to my ear. Something doesn't sound right. He's hiding something, but why? Is he hiding it because he is being recorded and doesn't want to admit to any more crimes? Or is he hiding it for some ulterior motive.

"I need you to come here, Olive," Owen says after a moment. "I need to see you. I need to tell you something in person."

"What?" I ask.

"It's something I can't say over the phone."

"They record the in-person conversations as well," I point out.

"I know, but—"

"Listen," I interrupt him. "I know what you're doing. It's just a ploy to get me out of here."

"I lied," Owen says after a moment. I wait for an explanation.

"I don't need to tell you something in person. I need you to come here and testify at my parole hearing."

My mouth drops open.

"They just told me after I hung up with you. That's why I called back."

"Congratulations," I say after a moment.

"Thank you."

Getting parole is a long shot but, in prison, it's important to celebrate every good thing that comes your way.

It doesn't mean you're jinxing yourself or setting yourself up for some disappointment, it's about being in the present.

The Department of Corrections gave Owen's case a once-over and he qualified for a hearing before the board.

Under any other circumstances, I

would be jumping up and down and doing everything short of throwing him a party over the phone. But today...I can't.

"I'm sorry," I catch myself. "I didn't mean to just gloss over it. It's a really big deal, Owen. I'm really happy for you."

"Thank you. I'm happy, too."

"You should've led the conversation with that, though," I point out. "You kind of buried the lead."

We stay on the phone for a few minutes. I wish more than anything that we hadn't talked about Nicholas and he hadn't told me any of those things.

I don't want to bring it up again and force another lecture.

I just want all of that stuff to disappear.

But that's not what life is about, is it? No matter how much you want to wish something away, it doesn't go away without you actually doing something about it.

"Please come," Owen pleads.

"When is it?"

"Two days from now."

"What?" I gasp.

"They had some sort of glitch in the

system. They were supposed to notify me sooner but they didn't. That's all I know."

"Are they even going to let me in?" I ask, thinking back to the one time when I drove all the way up to the prison, woke up in the dark, got in line to wait to come inside with the rest of the wives and girlfriends of the incarcerated only to be turned away for no reason.

They didn't let Owen have visitors that week but no one cared to notify either Owen or myself, even though I had registered to come.

I have been to that prison a dozen times since but it still irks me the way the guards treat the visitors, as if we are the convicts as well, as if we had done something wrong.

"They said that they will take a statement from someone on my side. I'd like that person to be you," Owen says.

"I don't know," I say, shaking my head. "I don't know if I can get back in time."

"Will you try?"

I nod.

"Olive? Will you try?"

18

WHEN I RUN AWAY...

This time, when I hang up, I put the phone on the table and leave it there. Rain which had been threatening to come down all morning finally lets loose.

Water falls in a loud steady stream, interrupted only by bolts of lightning and rolling waves of thunder.

I look at the way the rain pounds the big green bush, the name of which I don't know, right on the porch. When I open the door, my senses are overwhelmed by an intoxicating aroma of hot, wet vegetation.

I put my foot out past the awning and it immediately becomes soaked. I put it back and then stick my hand out.

Droplets run off my fingertips as if they were rain gutters.

I take a few steps forward and open my face up to the sky.

I welcome the beads of water that smash into me and even stick my tongue out.

"What are you doing?" His voice sounds muffled and originates somewhere in the distance.

I stand up straight and spin on my heels to face him. Nicholas, dressed in a casual Hawaiian shirt and khaki pants, is holding a large umbrella over his head.

"Just enjoying the warm rain," I say. "Haven't you ever done this?"

"Not recently. C'mon," he says, walking past me into my cottage. "I have to talk to you about something."

The air-conditioning feels cool on my skin and goose bumps immediately cover my body.

My clothes are soaked.

I step out of my soggy flip-flops. Nicholas gets a towel in the bathroom and hands it to me. I use it to wipe my face and dry my hair. The towel is too fat to pile on top of my head.

"Do you want to change?" he asks, sitting down on the couch in the living room. "I'll wait."

It's a request that's in the form of a question. Not long ago, I found this to be incredibly charming and not at all threatening. But knowing what I know now...I am not so sure.

I go to the other room and change into another long sleeve shirt and a cropped pair of yoga pants.

When I come out, I see Nicholas at my computer. My account has logged out but the screen is still up.

"Who do you know in prison?" he asks.

I crack my knuckles.

"Why are you looking through my stuff?" I ask.

"I wanted to check what the weather will be tomorrow. I forgot my phone back at the house."

His explanation is plausible enough the way that good explanations typically go.

I consider lying, pretending that it's

someone else I know who is in prison but what if I told him truth? Would that turn the tables? Would it catch him off guard?

"My brother, Owen, is doing a stretch for an armed robbery charge," I say.

My chest swells with pride using the right lingo just like the incarcerated do.

"Do you know him?" I ask.

The question slips out before I have a chance to really consider it. His eyes snap back and focus on mine. His face remains blank, devoid of all expression.

"Your brother?" he asks, buying more time. I nod and wait.

"Same last name? Owen Kernes?"

Again, I nod and wait.

"No." He shakes his head. "I don't think I do."

Our eyes remain locked on each other. He lies so effortlessly it makes my skin crawl.

"Why, did he say something?"

"No, not at all." I shake my head trying to be as nonchalant as he is.

Nicholas invites me back to his house for some dinner and I feel compelled to go.

I don't have any plans with Sydney and he knows full well that I have nothing else to do. We both have to eat. Plus, I don't want to raise any suspicion.

As we devour the meal that his chef has prepared, we don't speak.

My thoughts focus on the way his body tensed up just a bit when I asked about Owen. I don't know if that means anything, or if I'm just reading too much into everything. Still I can't shake this feeling that he's lying.

There isn't another Nicholas Crawford from that area of Boston. And there's definitely not one who steals valuables by making replicas first. Owen knew his original last name. He knew too much about him for this to not be the same person. Then there's the flinch.

When I asked him if he knew him, his shoulders tightened. He tried to cover it up. He took his time answering me. Those were all signs of deception.

"I have to go back to Boston tomorrow," I say, biting into the end of an asparagus spear.

"Tomorrow? Why?"

"I'm going to be a character witness for Owen at his parole hearing."

"Did you know about this before?" he asks, taking his time chewing every last bit of his arugula before bringing his fork up to his mouth with another bite.

"No, I just talked to him today. He didn't know before either. They were supposed to notify him but apparently he never got the message."

Nicholas takes a sip of his whiskey.

"Why aren't you saying anything?" I ask after a moment.

"Just trying to give you the opportunity to reach your own conclusion."

"About this," he says, taking another sip. I furrow my brow.

"I don't know understand what you don't understand," I say, taking a more stern approach. "I am not asking your permission. I am just notifying you about what I'm going to do."

Nicholas takes another bite. And then another. Then he finishes his drink and pours himself another. Still, he doesn't talk.

I put my plate in the sink and head toward the door.

"How are you going to get back to Boston?" he asks. "On what money?"

"I have enough for a ticket, don't worry about it."

"And what about our...arrangement? You promised to be at my disposal."

I slip into my flip-flops by the entrance and turn around to face him.

"I don't understand why you are making this so difficult," I say. "Don't you get what's going on here? My brother who has served years in prison finally has a chance to get out."

"Most inmates don't get parole during their first hearing," he points out.

I want to smack him across the face for saying that but instead I just ball up my fists.

"You're an asshole for saying that."

He shrugs.

"You know what, I can't talk to you when you have that smug expression on your face. Why don't you find me when you aren't so closed off."

I swing the front door open and step onto the porch. Water is falling in sheets but I have made too much of a scene to not leave.

"You're going to get soaked!" he yells so that I will hear him over the rain.

"I'm not made of sugar!" I scream back.

19

WHEN WE PLAY A GAME...

I'm about halfway down toward my cottage when he catches up to me. He grabs me by my arms from behind.

I fight to break free, but he holds me tightly. At first, I'm incensed.

Upset.

But the more we struggle, the more aroused I get.

He towers over me, clasps me firmly. I have nowhere to go and that's the way I want it.

When he spins me around, I stand on my tiptoes and press my lips to his. The kiss catches him by surprise, but it only takes a moment for him to respond in kind. His mouth opens wide, welcoming me in.

His arms release their grasp. But instead of pushing me away from him, they now pull me close.

I run my fingers up his neck and bury them in his hair. It is thick and soft even though it is completely waterlogged.

His hands get lost in my own mane. They go in circles and then pull down just as his tongue rushes into my mouth craving to intertwine with mine.

Wrapped in each other's arms, we let the rain fall onto us. To move or go back to a drier place would be to break the spell. Neither of us is ready for that yet.

His fingers grab my shoulders and then sweep down my arms. Another move and they are on the small of my back. I press my mouth harder against his. With our chests together, I can hear the thunder of our combined heartbeats.

Nicholas leads me back to my cottage. As soon as we are somewhere dry, he pushes me against the nearest wall.

His body is solid and defined. Muscles

protrude against his shirt, which he quickly peels off.

I run my fingers down his six pack, as he flexes and gives me a wink.

Licking his lips, he pushes me into the wall again. It's cold and smooth against my back. Then he starts to undress me.

A moment later, I'm in nothing but my bra and panties. He takes a step back to get a good look at me.

He objectifies me and it feels damn good. He wants me and he wants my body. As much as I want his.

I grab onto his belt and unbuckle it.

His pants fall to the floor and he tosses them to one side.

I look down at his substantial package. It's throbbing through his boxer briefs, which are so tight that I can see the vein running down it.

He's the biggest man I've ever been with. It's the size of the ones I've only seen in porn.

"You like?" he asks.

I nod.

My tongue finds the corner of my

mouth and slowly slides along the
bottom lip.

"I like, too," he says, grabbing the front
of my bra and unclasping it with one quick
move.

My breasts fall open for him. My
nipples stand up erect, waiting for him to
devour them.

He takes one in his mouth.

I press my head to the wall, enjoying
the sensation.

His tongue is hard but his mouth is soft,
filling the space between my legs with heat.

After pulling down my panties, he takes
my hand and leads me to the bed.

This is it.

No more foreplay.

No more games.

Just thrust yourself in me and fill me up
like no man has ever filled me up before.

I lie down on my back.

He climbs on top of me. He's naked
now, too.

When his body touches mine, I run my
fingers down his muscular back and then
toward his butt.

I take two big handfuls of his glutes and squeeze hard.

My legs open for him and wait.

Hovering slightly above me, he doesn't make a move to get any closer. I open my eyes.

"What are you waiting for?" I ask.

"You," he says without missing a beat.

"What do you mean?"

"If you want me to fuck you, you have to beg," he says, with a smug crooked smile on his face.

I furrow my brows and cock my head.

"Are you serious?" I ask.

Pulling himself away, he lies down next to me and props up his head. "I'll accept a please, or a pretty please. But you have to ask for it. Demand it even."

"No," I say, shaking my head.

"A promise is a promise," Nicholas says, his eyes lighting up. "You don't beg. You don't get this."

I grab the sheet and cover myself up.

"Get over yourself," I say, twisting away from him and turning off the lights.

20

WHEN HE MAKES ME CRY...

I wrap my sheet around my chest and prop up my head. My eyelids feel heavy, but I try to keep them open. Waves of emotion are no longer taking me on a rollercoaster ride. I look at him, but really somewhere past him in the distance.

Nicholas is just as relaxed. He lies flat on his back with his arm tucked behind his head. His hair is infused with body but not a mess. He stares at the ceiling. His chin is tilted upward, away from his body, as his chest moves up and down with each deep breath.

I have met my match. He wants me as much as I want him. We lust after each other, and yet, neither of us can give up the game. I will not beg and he will not give in until I do.

"So, are we actually ever going to *do* it?" I ask, teasing him.

"That's up to you," he says without moving a muscle.

"Oh, is it?"

"You ask me to, I comply and send you to the moon."

"Or the next time, you can just *not* stop," I suggest.

He turns to his side. His eyes focus on mine. After a bit, I'm the one who blinks first.

"So, there will be a next time?" he jokes.

"Maybe. Maybe not," I say smugly.

But if we keep talking like this, I can't be too sure that it won't happen again really soon.

I've never thought of myself as a competitive person but Nicholas seems to bring out that side of me.

Especially when it comes to this. He had set up the rules. When I agreed, the rules made me feel safe.

But now, I feel anything but that. Every time I touch his arm, every time he brushes up against me, the bolt of electricity that surges through me makes me weak in the knees.

It's almost as if my body aches for his and there's nothing I can do to keep that sensation at bay.

I lie back and look up at the ceiling tiles, which have thick crown molding around each one.

I've never seen anything like this except in magazines. As much as I want to keep them out, Owen's warnings about Nicholas and his true identity creep back in. He lied to me about not knowing my brother, and Owen wouldn't have any reason to lie.

But does knowing that change anything about our deal? I'd suspected that he had a past, with his skills, it would've been ignorant not to.

But what about the people that he has supposedly killed. Did he do it or are those just rumors?

"I have to go back to Boston," I say definitively.

Nicholas doesn't reply.

"I have to testify on my brother's behalf. He's all I have."

Again, Nicholas doesn't reply.

"If I don't go and he doesn't get out, I will never forgive myself."

He doesn't say a word.

"Are you listening to me?" I ask.

"I can't let you go," he says after a moment. There's that possessiveness rearing its ugly head.

"I don't need your permission," I remind him.

"You do, if you want to get paid. If you want to stick to the terms of our arrangement."

I sit up.

I feel tears of frustration and anger welling up in my eyes.

I had just quit my job.

The money he's offering me is more money than I will ever make in a lifetime. But is he really going to make me choose between all of that and my brother?

"I don't understand why you're making this so difficult. I can fly there and fly back right away. I will only stay there for the hearing."

Nicholas says nothing. His face is expressionless and empty. He continues to lie on his back staring at the ceiling. I touch his arm to try to shake him out of his trance, but again he doesn't respond.

"Why? Why can't I go? Our arrangement will remain the same. This is just a two day trip on a personal matter."

"You don't have the option to take personal days," Nicholas says slowly. "This isn't a normal job. If it were, then you would be paid normal money."

I get off the bed and take the sheet with me.

It slides off his naked body but he remains motionless. The muscles in his stomach move up and down with each breath. His legs lay slightly apart, relaxed.

His calmness makes me even more agitated. When it reaches a boiling point, I grab my pillow and toss it in his direction.

"What the hell is wrong with you?" I demand to know. "Why are you such a robot?"

Nicholas turns his head only slightly in my direction.

"What do you want to talk about?"

"I'm going to Boston," I say.

"Fine. Go."

He rises out of the bed and pulls on his trousers.

"What does that mean?" I ask, as he buckles the belt.

"It means we're done," he says. "I will buy you your ticket home and you will never hear from me again."

"Why?" I ask.

"Because I don't need you," he says harshly. His words are like a knife through my heart. My body trembles.

"But what about...the offer? Why did you even ask me here?"

He puts on his shirt. His hands are slow and meticulous, pushing every button through its designated loop.

"I thought we could help each other out," he says, finally meeting my eyes. "I thought we could have fun doing it. But I see now that you were never committed to me."

Still grasping onto my sheet, I walk up to him and grab him by his shoulders.

"I am committed. To you. To this deal. I just need a day. He's my brother and he has been in prison for years. This is his chance and if there's anything I can do to help him get parole...I have to do it."

"If it means giving up a million dollars?" Nicholas challenges me.

"I will do everything you want. Why do I have to?" I plead.

"Because I said so," he says.

21

WHEN I HAVE TO MAKE A CHOICE...

Hot tears start to stream down my face. I can barely see a thing through them. Nicholas doesn't put his arm around me. He doesn't comfort me in any way. The man that created so much heat inside of me now fills me with nothing but ice.

How could he do this?

Who is he?

Why is he doing this?

What is the big deal with me taking this short trip? Why is he being so unreasonable? The questions keep coming but the answers stay away.

"You have to make a choice, Olive," Nicholas says, walking up to me. He touches my chin and pulls it up to his eyes. "It's either Owen or me."

"Don't you see how ridiculous this is?" I ask. "I don't need to make a choice, you are making me. Why? Why are you being so...unreasonable?"

"I have my reasons," Nicholas says.

"Please," I beg. "You wanted me to plead, you wanted me to demean myself, to beg. I'm begging you now."

"I never wanted you to do anything you didn't want to do," he corrects me. "It's offensive that you think I wanted you to demean yourself."

I don't say a word.

Even though he is trying to remain calm, I see anger building up within him. I have finally gotten through.

He takes a deep breath.

His icy demeanor returns.

He only gave me a glimpse, but now it's gone.

He walks toward the door. I run after him and trip over my feet. I let go of the sheet that's wrapped around me but it's too late. The fabric is taut and it pulls me down to the floor.

"Nicholas, please," I say. I rise up to my feet and stand before him naked and totally vulnerable. "Can we talk about this?"

"There's nothing to talk about," he says.

"I want to spend the year with you. I want to go with you wherever you want to take me."

"But?" he finishes my thought.

"There is no but. That's the end of the sentence."

"What about Boston?"

I shrug. He knows my answer to that.

"Is there anything I can do to change your mind?" I ask. "I don't want this offer to be off."

Nicholas is about to say something but then he shakes his head. I can see that something is on the tip of his tongue, but what?

His lips open again and then purse shut.

"What? What is it?"

"It's...too dangerous."

"What are you talking about?" I ask.

"No." He shakes his head. "You should go back to Boston and our relationship is over."

"You have to tell me," I say, putting my hands on my hips.

I have never been so naked and felt so clothed before. It's like my nudity no longer exists.

This is who I am and this is what I look like. You can take it or leave it.

"If there's anything I can do, please tell me," I ask again.

He looks me up and down, I freeze.

But then I realize that he's not really scrutinizing me. Instead, he's gazing somewhere past me at nothing in particular. Thinking.

Am I really getting through to him?

"I have a job to complete. There's a dangerous man that I am after who has taken something very dear from me."

I nod.

"He was supposed to be at the party when we ran into Sydney and James."

A wave of relief starts to sweep over me.

I don't know where this story is going or what it will require me to do but at least we are talking.

At least, me going to testify at Owen's hearing is now a possibility.

"He is staying on the island tonight. He called a number to ask for an escort to be sent to his room," Nicholas explains.

My throat cinches up. I rub my index finger on my hip bone but remain motionless. He cannot see fear in my eyes. Then he will never let me do it.

"I've intercepted the call and I know that he's expecting her there at eight."

"What do you want me to do?" I ask, raising my chin in the air.

"No," he says, shaking his head. "This is a bad idea. I will just have to track him down and try again. It's too dangerous."

"I'm fine with dangerous," I say as bravely as I can. "Anything I can do to help." What I really mean is that I will do anything to prove to you that I'm in.

He hesitates.

I watch him think, analyze, assess the situation.

"If you do this, then I will take you to the prison to testify. But you have to stay by my side the whole time. You will not leave my side and you will not question my decisions."

I furrow my brow. He tilts his head toward mine waiting for an answer. I'm not sure I can get anything more out of this negotiation so I agree.

Without another word, he walks back to the front door, leaving me standing in the middle of the room, unsure as to what to do.

"Get dressed and come with me," Nicholas says. "I need to make sure you know what you're getting into before you agree to do this."

I swallow hard and put on my clothes.

I follow him to the main house and into one of the guest rooms.

Nicholas opens the large armoire and pulls out a hanger.

"You will have to wear this," he says.

To say that it's a bra and a pair of underwear would be a grave understatement. The cups are cut out completely, leaving nothing but straps. The panties are low rise bikini bottoms but also missing that ever important area that covers the crotch.

"Can you wear this?" Nicholas asks.

22

WHEN WE MAKE A PLAN...

I take the lingerie into my hands and examine it closely. The lace and the stitching is exquisite and expensive. The back of the panties is nothing but a long string.

"Why this?" I ask.

"He requested that the escort show up wearing this."

"So...you want me to have sex with him?" I ask, trying to hide the disappointment in my voice.

"No. Absolutely not," he says quickly. "I don't want him within a mile of you let alone touching you."

My heart swells a bit.

He does care about me.

Nicholas sits down on the bed.

I find a spot next to him.

"What is this? You have to talk to me," I say.

"No, this is a very bad idea," he says after a moment. "I can't let you do this."

"Why?"

"This guy is not anyone you want to mess with. He has killed a lot of people."

"What do you need to get back from him?" I ask.

"Something valuable."

I wait for him to continue but he doesn't.

"You're not going to tell me anything more than that?" I push.

"Not now."

When Nicholas gets up to pace around the room, I pick up the hanger with the lingerie and stare at it. There are lace and straps but to call it a complete *outfit* would be a grave understatement.

Still, if this is the only way I can get back to Owen and keep my end of the deal, it's worth it.

I quit my job.

After just two weeks of this, I'll get almost forty-two thousand dollars in cash. After a month, I'll have over eighty-three thousand. That's more than I would have made at my old job in a year.

And if I'm still with him for three hundred and sixty-five days, I'll have a million dollars. Cash.

That's enough to set me up for life. It's not about never working again, of course I will work. I love working. But it's about doing something that I'm really passionate about. Maybe I'll finally get that Masters or PhD in mathematics, anything other than write assessment items.

It's also about never worrying about bills again. So, if that requires me to wear this for one evening and not have sex with this guy...why not?

"What's the plan, Nicholas?" I ask. "I need to know what I have to do."

Nicholas stops mid-step and looks back at me.

"You show up in his hotel room. You distract him, make small talk. That will give me the opportunity to let myself in and take what I need. He's staying in the suite so you can lead him to the bedroom. What I'm looking for should be on the desk in the living room."

"Should I leave the door open for you?" I ask. What if I can't, I think to myself.

"You won't have to, I have the master key."

"You really planned this out."

"For bigger jobs like these, there are a lot of moving parts. On the back end."

I bite the inside of my mouth. There is so much I don't know about him and his line of work. But I'm kind of eager to find out.

"What happens then?" I ask. "After you take what you need to take?"

"I leave," Nicholas says.

"What about me?"

"You will receive a call and then make an excuse and leave as well."

"It sounds too easy," I say.

"It won't be," Nicholas assures me. "You will have to play a role. You will have to read him. Put him at ease. Then let yourself out without hurting his pride or his ego."

"And what if something goes wrong?" I ask.

"That's when we go to plan B. I really don't want to do plan B."

Again, I wait for him to explain but talking to him about this is like pulling teeth. He gives me the bare minimum of information and that's nowhere near enough.

Whenever I did my previous jobs, I always made sure that I thought of at least five escape plans; things I would say and things I would do in case A, B, C, D, and E happened.

This isn't how I operate.

I'm going into this blind and it doesn't feel safe.

But I don't have much of a bargaining position if I want to hold on to the deal we made. I can see him hesitating about getting me involved. He wants this thing that he took but he's wondering if the risk is too great.

"Nicholas, I need to know more. I need

to know what his suite looks like. What he's like. I need to know what I'm getting myself into so I can protect myself against him in case anything happens."

Nicholas swallows hard.

"If anything happens, you won't be able to protect yourself. That is the *fucking* problem. That's why this is such a bad idea."

He starts to pace again.

His body makes short, jerky movements.

He rubs the back of his neck. Closing his eyes, he takes a calming breath and turns to face me.

"No," he says after a moment. "This isn't a good idea. Too many things can go wrong."

"But you had everything planned out."

"I don't. You are right. I don't know the layout of that hotel room. I don't know anything about him but his first name. Jobs are only successful when you are prepared. I was prepared back there in the club. I had intel that he was going to bring the laptop with him and leave it in his locker. He always felt safe there."

Laptop.

The word slips out of his mouth before he realizes what he's saying. Nicholas and I make eye contact.

No, it wasn't a slip.

Nothing with him is by accident.

He wanted to tell me so he did.

"This is a good plan. I'll distract him while you go in and take the computer," I insist. "You were planning on switching it? You already have a replica, right? A laptop that's identical in every way except one."

I want to ask him what's on it but that's not important now. What's vital is to go through with the plan so I can get back for the parole hearing.

"It doesn't look like it but I'm good with people. Small talk, that kind of thing. I'll put him at ease," I lie. "I'll take him to the bedroom, everything will be fine."

I'm so positive and confident that I manage to convince myself that this job is going to be no different from walking into a department store and taking a dress off the rack.

I ask Nicholas to lay out all of the details.

He shows me the laptop.

He tells me the name of the hotel. The guy's room number.

I already know the time that I'm supposed to be there.

It sounds like he's starting to ease into this plan. It sounds like he is starting to believe that it's, in fact, possible for us to get away with it. But then he throws a bombshell.

"No, absolutely not," Nicholas says. "I'm not letting you do this."

23

WHEN THE PLAN CHANGES...

I try to change his mind for a bit longer but then give up. There's no use. He has made his final decision.

Angry and upset, I go back to my cottage.

It's seven o'clock. I only have one hour before the deal is officially off. My mind starts to race.

I'm in free fall and my adrenaline is on high. A nagging thought keeps popping up in the back of my mind. *What if I do this by myself?*

I don't need Nicholas' permission. I have done plenty of jobs entirely only my own. Now, he knows only a little bit about my past but he doesn't trust me.

If I were to do this and get the laptop to him then it will take our professional relationship to a whole new level.

I sneak back to the main house.

I hear falling water and I know he's taking a shower. I open the drawer where he keeps the laptop and place it into my backpack.

Tiptoeing into the guest bedroom, I grab the lingerie off the hanger and stuff it into my pockets. The shower stops and I freeze for a moment, holding my breath.

Snap out of it, I say to myself, forcing myself to focus. The worst thing you can do in a situation like this is to do nothing.

On the console table near the front door, in a porcelain bowl, I see five pairs of car keys.

The door creaks.

There's no time left. I grab the first one and carefully turn the knob so that it makes the least amount of sound possible. Once I'm on the other side, I close it with the same meticulousness.

I slip down the stairs.

Running my fingers along the house and sticking as close as possible to the siding, I make my way to the garage.

Luckily, it's open and there are a number of cars parked right in the front. I click the button on the key chain, pointing to one car at a time.

A silver Mercedes responds.

I climb in, press the accelerator, and drive out slowly, praying that Nicholas doesn't hear me.

I arrive at the hotel five minutes before eight. After being barefoot since I walked up the stairs to Nicholas' door, the wedges that I got from Marshall's feel heavy and cumbersome.

I say hello to the valet and walk straight to the bathroom in the lobby.

First rule of a good con, if you want to act like you belong somewhere then act like you do.

I don't look around.

I don't look like I have any questions.

I hold my head up high. I have to look

like I know exactly what I'm doing even if I don't have a clue.

The stalls are all empty. I consider using the one meant for disabled people or families with the changing table. Since I don't fit into either category, I decide against it.

Second rule of a good con, never break unnecessary rules and regulations.

Never speed.

Never park in the wrong place.

Never use a stall not meant for you.

It may not seem like a big deal but it's little things like these that will come back to haunt you later on.

I change out of my clothes in the smaller stall, stuffing my other clothes into the backpack that I hang on the hook above.

Once I clasp the bra in the back, I look down and bounce my naked breasts in the air. The space between my legs is equally unsupported by the crotchless underwear. I wrap myself up in the trench coat and apply a coat of red lipstick in front of the floor length mirror.

"You can do this," I say to myself.

I stretch out my fingers as a rush of excitement courses through me.

I should be afraid but instead I'm strangely turned on.

Perhaps, it's the lingerie or how amazing it makes me feel.

I've never worn anything like this before.

It makes me feel sexy and alluring. The only disappointing thing is that Nicholas won't be the first person to see me dressed in this.

When I knock on his door, I take a step back noting that familiar feeling I had every time I took something that didn't belong to me.

It's difficult to explain to someone who hasn't ever done it, except to say that it feels dangerous and exciting at the same time.

Your breathing speeds up. Your pulse rate goes through the roof, but your hand remains still.

Calm.

Under control.

The man who answers isn't who I

expect. Even though Nicholas told me that he has killed before, I still assumed he would be kind of meek, small, maybe even bald and unattractive. This man is nothing like that. He's tall, with broad shoulders, an expensive haircut, and a cut body.

Dressed in a tight white t-shirt, he gives me a young Marlo Brando vibe circa *A Streetcar Named Desire*. He even smells manly.

"Dallas Stone," he says, looking me up and down.

"Abigail Sanders," I say, giving him a strong handshake.

Touching his jaw and licking his lips, I can see that he likes the way I look. I let out a little sigh of relief and walk into the living room.

With his eyes burning holes in my ass, I look around the suite.

There's a couch to one side and a small worktable on the far end.

The laptop sits squarely in the middle with the lid closed.

"Would you like a drink, Abigail?" Dallas asks.

"Yes, please, vodka with spritzer water and a wedge of lemon."

Dallas goes over to the bar.

"Do you go by Abigail or Abby?" he asks, cutting the lemon.

"Abigail," I say.

I practiced the name earlier in the car so that when I said it out loud it would come off as natural as my own name.

"What should I call you?"

"Dallas for now," he says. "Mr. Stone later."

I turn around to let him see my eyes light up.

My mouth forms a little smile.

The thing is that it's not all an act. I'm strangely attracted to him.

Well, maybe there's nothing strange about it.

He oozes sex and he knows it. There's an arrogance to him in the way he is already undressing me with his eyes.

My tongue touches the roof of my mouth when I have a dirty thought. He looks like a good lay. What if I were to fuck him first?

24

WHEN THERE'S AN
INTERRUPTION...

Dallas gives me the drink and I take a sip. It's slow and deliberate. I lick my lips and enjoy him watching me do it.

I know that I should be scared, but I'm not.

I'm here to do a job, but would it be so terrible if I had a little fun along the way? I don't owe Nicholas a thing. We have a professional relationship and I want to have sex with him as well but he's playing games with me. And two can play this game.

Another part of me is angry with Nicholas.

I'm pissed off that he was so

unreasonable as to forbid me to go back to Boston and help my brother.

Who the hell does he think he is?

What gives him the right?

I look Dallas up and down. Maybe fucking him is the best thing for me. I haven't been with a man for a while now, all of the way that is, and this guy may be just what I need.

The fact that it will also go a long way to piss off Nicholas would just be the icing on the cake.

I take another sip and take a step toward Dallas.

The glass makes a loud clinking sound when it touches the marble table.

I'm so close to him, I smell his minty fresh breath.

I appreciate the preparation.

"What would you like to do with me?" I ask slowly.

His eyes are blue, the color of the ocean, with flecks of green.

"Something bad," he says after a moment.

Reaching over, I run my fingers up his

neck and along his jawline.

He takes a step forward and kisses me on the mouth.

His lips are demanding. They part mine and immediately make their way inside.

His hands pull on the belt of my trench coat. Then he pulls away from me.

"You want to see?" I ask, raising one eyebrow.

He nods with a wide smile.

I grab it by the lapels and toss it off me.

I stand before him exposed.

Naked but not naked at the same time.

His eyes slowly leave mine and travel down my elongated neck, down toward my chest.

They pause as he looks at my nude breasts before looking further down.

I suck in my stomach a bit and stand up as straight as possible. This should be Nicholas' eyes on my body, but Dallas's will do for tonight.

My pulse speeds up as I anticipate all the bad things he will do to me while I imagine that he is Nicholas.

He's about to say something but I beat him to it.

I spread my legs in a wider stance, for him to take a better look at the apex of my thighs.

Then when I think he has had enough I turn around and fold my body in half.

Keeping my arms straight, I place my hands on my knees and extend my butt outward and into the air. I feel his eyes on my body and a warmness starts to radiate from my core.

He takes a step toward me and runs his fingers up my thighs.

My legs open wider for him, aching to be touched, but instead of pulling them inside of me, he wraps them around the cheeks of my ass and goes up the sides toward my breasts.

I stand up straight.

Cupping both of them at the same time, he presses his body to mine with the bulge of his pants directly on my coccyx.

It's thick and wide and it feels like it's made of wood.

Grinding my butt against it, my thoughts return to Nicholas.

If only he were to see us now.

If only he were to be forced to watch, unable to stop a thing.

My imagination is so vivid, I can almost taste his jealousy.

A knock on the door forces him to pull away. I wipe the sweat off my palms on my thighs.

Maybe it's just room service.

Maybe it's nothing to worry about.

From where I'm standing, I have a clear view of the door.

It's a beautiful woman.

"Oh, hey! I didn't realize that they were going to send both of us," I say, taking two large leapfrog jumps toward them.

"Um...I thought..." the woman starts to say.

I interrupt her by reaching toward her and pulling her inside.

"The more the merrier, right?" I ask, raising one eyebrow and biting my lower lip. I drape myself over both Dallas and the woman.

The escort is a natural at playing characters so she quickly puts her bag on the counter and starts to undress.

But Dallas rubs the back of his neck, concerned.

"Looks like I have some catching up to do," she jokes, turning around for him to unclasp her bra.

Do it.

Do it. Do it, I say silently to myself.

He reaches for the straps instead and pushes them off her shoulders. By the time I see her nipples, Dallas's face relaxes and he starts to believe.

I let out a little sigh of relief.

That was close.

But now...I have another problem.

The escort has Pantene commercial hair with legs that go on for miles. Her booty is as perky and perfect as her breasts.

Still, I have never even kissed a girl and my desire for Dallas has evaporated with the prospect of getting caught.

It's not that she isn't sexy. It's more like whatever trance I was just under has vanished and I know that the best thing to do is to get the job done and get the hell out of here.

Dallas gets down on his knees and puts her breasts in his mouth.

"C'mon, join us," he mumbles and waves me over.

I glance over at the table with the laptop.

My bag with the copy is all the way across the room. This is going to be quite a challenge.

Focus, I say to myself. You can do this. Just think.

It's not a problem unless there is a solution.

And there's a solution here.

"Let's move over to the bed," I suggest.

25

WHEN HE SURPRISES ME...

I walk over to the bedroom and stand with my legs and arms apart holding on to the two French doors. The sections of each door are made of glass but luckily, they are also covered in curtains for a semblance of privacy.

"You must be new," the escort says. "I don't think I've caught your name."

My heart drops. Dallas can't suspect that I'm not who I say I am.

"I'm not new," I say, taking my finger and running it down one of her breasts. When I reach her nipple, I give it a little pinch. "I just switched over from another outfit. I'm Abigail."

"It's a pleasure," she says, opening her mouth and grazing her tongue along the edge of her teeth. "I'm Rosemary."

"Okay, ladies, I'm ready," Dallas says, lying down spread eagle on his back.

"I don't think you are," Rosemary says, climbing onto the bed.

I wait a moment for them to lose themselves in each other's bodies.

"I'll be right there," I say. "My mouth is a desert."

That part is true.

I want to clear my throat, but I cover it with my hand instead to not mess with the mood.

I open the door and then quickly close it behind me, but not all of the way through so that the lock doesn't make a sound.

Once I'm outside, I don't waste any time.

I grab my bag, rush across the living room to the desk with his laptop and make the switch.

In the kitchen, I turn on the water in the sink to make it seem like I'm pouring myself a glass and then slip through the front door.

Holding the handle so that it doesn't make a sound as it closes behind me, I only let out a small sigh of relief once I get to the fire escape.

Running down the stairs, I put on my trench coat, only slowing down my gait when I reach the lobby.

"What are you doing here?" I ask when I run into him in the parking lot.

"Get in," Nicholas says from behind the wheel of his BMW.

"No, I drove your car here."

Without missing a step, I unlock my car and I get in.

My phone rings when I pull out of the hotel's parking lot and disappear down the winding highway along the coast.

"What the hell were you thinking?" He demands to know as soon as I answer.

"Thanks for sending in the other escort," I say sarcastically. "That made things a lot easier."

"You weren't supposed to go. The deal was off."

Anger starts to build up in the pit of my stomach.

"Who the hell do you think you are, talking to me like this?" I demand to know.

"I'm...I'm," he says, stumbling for the right word. "I'm your fucking boss."

"No, you're not. You're my partner."

"Oh, is that right?" he asks, his tone oozing in derision.

"Yes, that's right."

"The last time I checked, one partner usually doesn't arrange everything and pay the other a salary. Only a boss does that."

I hang up the phone, hitting my palms on the steering wheel. As expected, he calls back.

I don't answer.

He keeps calling. I refuse to answer.

After three attempts, he gives up.

I drive in silence around a few bends. The GPS lady on my phone warns me that I have to turn in 0.2 of a mile. That's the exit onto his property, but that's the last place I want to go right now.

When she tells me to turn, I keep going. She tells me to do a U-turn so I turn her off completely. Not going anywhere in particular, I press down on the accelerator.

I don't see Nicholas behind me and it seems like he either turned onto the road toward his house or just fell behind. Either way, I wait for a phone call but it doesn't come.

I take a few more turns around the cliffs before pulling onto a turnout and parking the car. There's a narrow path leading down to the beach. I make my way down carefully since I'm no expert in walking in heels, even if they are wedges.

The beach is wild and deserted.

It looks like man hasn't touched it in centuries.

The sand is soft but covered in naturally occurring debris.

I find a spot away from the splinters and driftwood. I pull my knees up to my face and rest my chin on top. I listen to the swishing of the water as it comes and goes in a continuous rhythm and then take off my shoes, burying my toes in the sand.

"I'm sorry," Nicholas says, walking over to me.

His voice breaks my concentration but doesn't frighten me.

"What do you want?" I ask.

"I want to apologize."

"For what?" I ask. "I thought you were never wrong."

This seems to hurt him, but that's exactly how I mean it.

I do want to inflict pain. I'm angry at him for following me here.

I'm angry at him for ruining my surprise. I'm angry at him for lecturing me as if I am a kid who did something wrong.

I turn my face toward him. Shrugging my shoulders and lifting my chin, I wait for him to talk.

"I'm sorry for saying that I'm your boss."

I nod.

"But...

"But what?" I ask. "You realize, of course, that this 'but' negates your whole apology."

"Well, that's not what I mean to do."

"Well, that's what *you are* doing," I say. "You're justifying and that means you're not really apologizing."

Nicholas sits down next to me.

"Why did you go there?" he asks.

I bite my lower lip and stare into the distance.

"I knew I could do it and I did," I say, sitting up straight.

"You did?" he asks.

By the tone of his voice, I can tell that something is different. Slowly, I turn my head toward him. His eyes are lit up like it is Christmas morning.

"That doesn't change anything," I point out.

"No, that's where you are wrong," he corrects me. "It changes everything!"

26

WHEN WE TALK...

Nicholas and I sit on the sand for a bit staring at the waves crashing just below our feet. There are so many things I want to ask him.

There are so many questions that I need answered.

Just not at this very moment.

I bury my hands in the sand. I bring my palms together and scoop up as much of it as I can.

"You calling that escort to go to his room didn't help much," I finally say. Nicholas' mouth drops open.

"What happened?" he whispers.

I prop up my head with my hand and

rest it on my knee.

"It kinda killed the mood," I joke.

He furrows his brows, looking perplexed.

"Dallas isn't a bad looking guy," I explain.

My lips form into a little smile that I can't force off my face.

"What are you talking about?" Nicholas asks.

I don't respond. He turns his body toward mine, grabbing me by my shoulders.

"Don't tell me you were thinking of... what exactly? Actually, going through with *it*?"

I shrug, reveling in his jealousy. "I was expecting some troll but he and I had real heat. Besides, I haven't had sex, proper sex, in a long time."

"You wanted to *fuck* him?" Nicholas asks.

"Yeah, maybe." I smile.

"Don't you know who he is?" he says, shaking his head.

"No, I don't. That's the problem. You

didn't tell me anything about him."

"That's because I wanted to protect you. I called this whole operation off."

I shake my head and turn away from him.

He forcibly turns my face toward him.

"What happened?" he asks.

The fire in his eyes is still there but it no longer feels like just jealousy. It's something more than that.

I go over the broad strokes.

"You're lucky that you slipped out of there when you did," Nicholas says.

This irritates me.

"I don't need you to tell me that. I'm not an idiot."

"I wasn't implying that you were."

Shaking my head, my eyes follow the seagull that wanders around the edge of the water looking for a snack.

When he puts his hand on my arm, I brush it away.

"I didn't want you to go because I was worried that something might go wrong and then..." Nicholas' voice trails off. "I didn't want anything to happen to you."

"What do you care?" I ask. "I'm just your employee."

"Why are you making this so hard?"

"Because you make me angry," I say. "You put me into an impossible position. You refused to let me go back home and be there for my brother."

"That wasn't fair," he says.

"You can say that again."

I don't know if he really doesn't understand or if he is just trying to be difficult, but the emotional rollercoaster that I have just experienced is all because of that choice.

"It wasn't really a choice. It was an unfair thing to ask me to do," I continue. "You know that. I don't have any other family but Owen. My mother is an asshole. She doesn't care about me or anyone else but her. She won't be there for him, and even if she were, what would she say? He's all I have."

"I'm sorry," Nicholas says quietly.

"When you suddenly and arbitrarily, mind you, decided that suddenly I wasn't experienced enough to do this job, I had to prove you wrong. I'm sorry I snuck out and stole your car but I did what I needed to do. I don't have a fucking job anymore and you are going to pay me my first paycheck if it's the last thing you do."

The words fly out of my mouth without much editing for content, meaning, or impact. It's almost as if they have a mind of their own.

"I was never *not* going to pay you," he says.

I let out a mocking chuckle.

Nicholas scooches over to me. Our arms touch. He turns his body to face mine. Placing his finger under my chin he turns my face toward his.

"There is still a lot you don't know about me," he says.

I meet his eyes and don't look away.

"But I always pay my debts."

"Okay," I say.

"Also..." He leans over and kisses me.

My mouth opens up to welcome him inside before my mind can stop it. He buries his hands in my hair. Shivers run down my body each time he tugs.

His lips are soft and powerful, devouring mine. Our tongues touch and intertwine. His hands make their way down my neck and to my back. They look for a way to my flesh, but I'm sitting on the bottom of my coat.

His hands find the belt and unwrap it moving quickly. When he pushes the sides of my coat off my shoulders and away from my body, he realizes that underneath I am dressed in that lingerie that he had showed me on the hanger.

His mouth waters and he licks his lips.

He positions himself right in front of me, and I spread my legs slowly for him.

My nipples get hard from the way he looks at them and the wind feels nice against the crease in between my thighs.

I'm completely exposed, surrounded by only the strings of the crotchless bikini, and now also somewhat covered in sand.

"Oh, wow," Nicholas whispers, taking off his own shirt. I run my fingers down his hard body, pausing briefly over each washboard ab.

Nicholas leans over and picks up my leg.

"Lie down," he says. "I want you to enjoy this."

I do as he says and close my eyes.

His lips make their way from my toes up to my knees. Then up around the outside of my thighs before dipping down on the inside.

My body throbs for his. I arch my back and open my legs even wider.

Touch me. Touch me down there. You know where, I say silently.

But he doesn't. Instead, he does the same thing up my other leg. When he reaches the inside of my thighs, his kisses get more frantically. My body burns for him even more. He reaches up, taking one of my breasts into his hand.

The other remains down below.

"I want you," I say. "Now."

He leans over me. His substantial package presses against my pelvic bone. I wrap my legs around him.

"Are you taking birth control?" he asks.

I was, but I've given it up. They always

made me feel kind of off and bloated and I haven't been having sex with anyone to make them worthwhile.

"No," I say.

"I don't have any condoms," he says.

He tries to kiss me again, but I stop him.

"I can't have sex without protection," I say.

That's a rule I haven't broken since I became old enough to have sex.

I'm terrified of getting pregnant by accident or possibly getting some sort of disease. No matter how aroused I have felt in the moment, I have never broken this rule.

When, or rather, if I ever get pregnant it will be because I want a child. There are enough unwanted children in this world and I know that I couldn't handle a baby that I didn't really want to have.

"I don't want to have sex without using anything either," Nicholas says, lying down next to me.

I turn on my side, laying one leg over the other and propping my head up with my hand. He mirrors my position. Scooping up a handful of sand, he slowly releases it onto my thighs.

Some of it blows away in the breeze, but most of the grains land and either go down the front or the back of my body.

I reach over and touch his penis. It's big and as hard as a rock. I unbuckle his shorts and he slides them off him.

I look at the large vein that runs the whole way down it and the way it moves every time I give it a little squeeze.

I wait for him to push me to do it anyway, even without protection, but he surprises me. He doesn't press.

Instead, he continues to play with my body, covering it in sand.

Laying me down on my back, he makes little mounds of sand on my stomach and in between my breasts.

The sexier he makes me feel, the harder I squeeze his penis. After a while, we both start to moan.

"I want to watch you pleasure yourself," he says.

His words send a shock of electricity through my body.

My legs open as if on their own. I touch my breasts and then quickly make my way toward the center of my body.

The sand feels rough, but I manage to flick off most of the grains as my fingers find their way inside. The pleasure forces my butt off the ground.

When my eyes drift over, I see that he's touching himself, too, watching me. His eyes are glued to my hands.

Watching him watching me pushes me over the edge. The warm sensation in the pit of my core spreads quickly throughout me. My hands move faster and faster and then a wave of exhilaration rushes over me. When I turn my eyes to Nicholas, his hips move faster and faster until he comes as well.

Afterward, we walk into the water, hand in hand and completely nude. The water isn't very warm, but my well-heated body welcomes the refreshment. Nicholas takes me into his arms and kisses me again.

Then he leans over and whispers, "This doesn't mean that you can go to Boston by yourself though."

27

WHEN HE SPEAKS...

The room smells like bleach and sharpened pencils. It reminds me of my sixth grade classroom, minus the wall decorations.

There are large plastic tables set up against the windows on the far end where the panel of judges sit. The parole board consists of four men and three women, all over the age of forty-five.

I don't know what requirements you have to possess to get yourself this position but none of them really look like they could relate to the kind of upbringing that Owen and I had.

The only advice that Owen gave me when I was trying to figure out what to say was to speak from your heart. Not exactly useful.

Owen sits at a table directly in front of me with his attorney. This isn't the same guy who represented him all of those years ago. After losing the case, that lawyer stopped returning his calls.

This one is a woman, who looks like she's barely out of high school. She has a meek voice and she's dressed in an outfit that's way too big for her small frame.

The parole panel speak among themselves in hushed tones. The way they shuffle papers back and forth makes me wonder if this is the first time that they are reviewing his case.

The guards brought Owen in twenty minutes ago and no one has spoken yet. Unlike the inmates on television, he is dressed in his usual garb; hunter green pants and a matching button-down shirt with a white t-shirt underneath.

He has short light brown hair, cut short,

as if he's in the armed forces. Before prison, he had always worn it long, and the first time I saw him with his new haircut I worried that he had been forced to join some Aryan Nation gang.

When I asked about it, he denied it. It's hard to know if the person on the other side of the plexiglass is ever telling the truth, so I would scan his body for tattoos hoping to find out the truth. No swastikas or other hate symbols appeared so I decided to take his words at face value.

Under the harsh fluorescent lights, everyone's skin is sallow and pale, including Owen's. But otherwise, he looks healthy. Well-rested even.

He gives me a big, white, toothy smile as soon as he sees my face. I know that no matter how long he spends in here, no matter how old we get, that smile will always remain the same. It will always belong to the happy go lucky little kid who never used to have a worry in the world.

Owen was convicted of armed robbery. He didn't stick up the liquor store but he was in the car waiting for his friends who did. This whole time he's maintained that he had no idea that they were going to do that.

They had all been drinking. After running out of alcohol, they drove down to the Five and Dime. It was after two a.m. and the cashier was busy watching television.

He didn't speak much English so his friends thought it would be funny to just take some stuff. They lined their pockets with chips and soda and anything else they could find.

They were laughing and joking around too loudly and the guy at the counter noticed that they were trying to sneak out. He pulled out a baseball bat and started yelling at them in Korean. Two of them dropped everything they had, but one of them pulled out a gun from his back pocket.

The video they showed in court didn't have sound, but it did capture the fear in the guy's face. Being a convenience store clerk on the graveyard shift is one of the most dangerous jobs in the world. Suddenly, the gun went off. The bullet missed the target and lodged itself in the wall behind the cashier.

After gathering the stuff they'd dropped onto the floor, they ran out and told Owen to drive. He didn't even know there had been the robbery. Of course, that's not the way the prosecutor had put it. To him, they had planned this whole thing out. They went in there to steal five packets of chips and four bottles of soda. And they were all in on the shooting. The jury gave them all the same sentence. If the cashier had been killed, Owen would have probably received life in prison.

After shuffling the documents in front of them from one person to another and familiarizing themselves with my brother's case, they give him the floor. One of them asks him to go over what happened that night.

I don't see why this is necessary, but Owen isn't fazed. He starts at around seven o'clock and the drinking.

"And why did you decide to stay behind

in the car?" the oldest parole board member asks.

Because it was freezing and he didn't want to leave the warm car or turn the engine off. That was what Owen always did whenever we went anywhere together. He hated running errands and would always prefer to stay inside the vehicle even if the shopping trip would take an hour.

"I had a hunch as to what might happen," Owen says.

My eyes open wide. What?

"Can you please elaborate?"

"It was late and we were all joking around and had been drinking quite a lot. No one mentioned doing it directly but I had my suspicions," he says.

"And you didn't want to stop them?"

"I wasn't sure. Those guys say a lot of things."

His attorney nudges him. She whispers something into his ear and he starts to elaborate. He tells them that they have never done anything like this but they were talking about it for a bit back at the house.

This answer isn't satisfactory. One of the members flips through his file and then asks, "Why did you say during the trial that you wanted to sit in the car because it was cold out?"

28

WHEN I SPEAK...

Because that's the *fucking* truth! I want to yell out and have to bite down on my tongue to stop myself. My hands start to tingle and I rub one with the other. My stomach feels heavy like I had just eaten a five-course meal even though I had nothing but a power bar this morning.

"My attorney told me to plead not guilty," Owen says and then stops himself. "No, I was pleading not guilty. And I lied."

"Do you often lie to get what you want, Mr. Kernes?" one of them asks. It takes actual effort to not run over there and smack that smug look off his face.

"No, I don't, but in that situation I did,"

Owen says, keeping his composure. "I was a kid. I was scared. I was facing a lot of time."

"It says here that the prosecutor did offer you a deal."

"It would've required me to testify against my friends and put them in jail for a very long time. I couldn't do that."

"What about now?"

"The trial is over. They are serving their time. This is a parole hearing and I want to be as honest as possible. I want to apologize to the Kim family for causing them all of this distress. I know that Mr. Kim must've suffered severe PTSD from going through what we put him through and I am very sorry for that. My apology doesn't come with any qualifications or explanations. I did a bad thing and that's what I have realized after all of this time in prison."

I put my hand over my racing heartbeat but it doesn't slow it down one bit.

Why is he saying all of these things?
After all of this time, why is he lying like this?

Then I answer my own question.

Of course. How could I be so stupid?

He's telling them what they want to hear.

If he comes up there and makes excuses for what he did or minimizes his role in the robbery then they will think that he hasn't learned his lesson.

It's a chess game and he's finally playing to win.

I can still remember how much my tears burned while I begged him to testify for the prosecution.

They were offering one year in jail and three years probation. I pleaded for him to take their deal. They had everything on video and the law on their side. He had waited for them in the car while they committed the robbery. That meant that he was as guilty of whatever they did as they were.

But Owen refused. It wasn't that he didn't believe that he would be convicted. It was more that he couldn't turn on his friends. But now that everything is said and done, now that he's at his first parole board hearing, he can speak as freely as he wishes. Or rather, he can tell them whatever they want to hear.

After Owen finishes his statement with another impassioned plea, it's my turn. I came here thinking that I would stand behind his old story one hundred percent and plead for them to let him go because he wasn't really part of what transpired.

But now, as I walk up to the front, I have no idea what I'm going to say.

My hands shake along with the rest of my body. I am thankful for the blazer that I wore over my button-down shirt.

With every step I take, I can feel the wetness under my arms spreading.

I have always been terrified of public speaking. Whenever I would see a podium set up in the classroom, my body would shut down and I would often pretend that I had some sort of illness. If I knew a speech was coming up, I would skip that class or school altogether. But right now, I wish to God I had a podium to lean on.

I stop in the middle of two tables. Owen and his attorney sit to my left and the prosecutor to my right. There are chairs set up behind the prosecutor for the Kim family but they are all empty.

I clear my throat and take a deep breath.

"I'm Owen's younger sister. He asked me to be here as a character witness," I start. That's all that I can use from my previous speech.

Shit!

Okay, focus. Just speak from the heart. But don't say too much that's contradictory with what he has just said.

Shit! Shit!

"I came here with everything that I was going to say memorized, but now I just want to tell you about my brother. We did not have the best childhood. Our eldest brother died in a car crash sending our mother, who wasn't much of a mother, into a downward spiral. Then our father went out to the store for milk and never came back. This crushed her even more and she stopped getting out of bed. She never really had a job or did any of the cooking or the shopping or cleaning so it was just us doing everything. I am not telling you this as an excuse for what Owen did, but I just want you to know what kind of world we were living in at the time. When Owen got older, he started hanging out with the wrong kind of people. There aren't very many good types of people running around the streets of Boston late at night. He was young and didn't think that anything could happen. Well, it did. I am very sorry to Mr. Kim and the rest of the Kim family for what happened. I know that he has suffered from post-traumatic stress disorder and I can imagine how hard it must've been for him to return to his job. My only consolation is that he was not physically hurt."

29

WHEN WE LISTEN TO HIM...

When I speak to them, I focus on their eyes so that they know that I am being genuine but I'm not really looking at them. More like through them.

It's a trick Nicholas told me about on the flight here. Looking into people's eyes while speaking terrifies me but avoiding eye contact will make me appear deceitful.

So, he told me to just look behind them. Through them and at some inanimate object right over their shoulder.

"As you can see, Owen is not here pleading his case," I continue. "He's not saying that he's not guilty. He's not trying to make you believe something that the jury didn't. He is telling you that he is guilty and that he is sorry for what happened. Very, very sorry. And that means that prison has taught him exactly what it was supposed to. It rehabilitated him."

My speech doesn't come to a close the way it goes in movies. It doesn't finish on an uplifting piece of music that tells the audience that the right side will prevail at the end. But I sit down with a quiet feeling of satisfaction nevertheless.

It's over. I have made my case.

I have pleaded for leniency and I did it off the cuff and from my heart.

The parole board continues to shuffle their papers and then it's the prosecutor's turn. Instead of focusing on who Owen is, his speech is more about the purpose of doing time.

"Prison has four purposes: retribution, incapacitation, deterrence, and rehabilitation," he says. "Owen Kernes sits before you, telling you everything that you want to hear. You don't want to hear excuses. You want him to give you a categorical apology. But the Kim family are not the only people who Mr. Kernes has hurt. He has committed a crime against society. He is a criminal, and depriving him of his freedom is the way to make him pay a debt to society for his crime."

What fucking crime? Sitting in the car while his idiot friend waves a gun around until it goes off? What exactly did he do that gives you permission to take his twenties away from him? And now you want even more?

"Incapacitation is the removal of criminals from society so that they can no longer harm innocent people. We did that with Owen, it is up to you to decide if we did it for long enough. Deterrence refers to preventing future crimes. Given Owen's upbringing and his past," the prosecutor says, "it is unclear whether prison will deter him to not commit crimes in the future. But if he remains incarcerated, you will be able to rest soundly at night."

I stare him down without trying to make it too obvious.

Who the hell does this guy think he is saying all of this shit? Making all of these assumptions. He doesn't know a thing about Owen, or our family, or what he will do a month from now, let alone a year from now.

I glance over at Owen whose expression remains calm and detached.

This isn't his first time in court and this isn't his first time being judged by complete strangers by a few sentences printed on pieces of paper.

After years of prison, he is used to it.

I, on the other hand, am not.

"Finally, we reach rehabilitation," the prosecutor says.

He doesn't need to state the definitions of any of these terms to either the parole board, the defense attorney, Owen, or anyone else in this room except maybe me.

But he does so for effect.

He uses these words to make a point and to prove it at the same time.

"The last but not least important purpose of our penal system is to rehabilitate criminals to make sure that they become law abiding citizens. As we all know, Owen has taken advantage of the opportunities that we offer. He learned to read and write and has gone far in his education. But as you take that into account, don't forget that with education comes knowledge. Knowledge as to how to manipulate the system and knowledge about what he should and shouldn't say to you to get what he wants."

So, in other words, there is no way to win.

If he hadn't learned to read, then you would be standing here saying that he hasn't taken advantage of any of the resources available to rehabilitate himself.

But now that he has, you are saying that he has done so only to advance his own agenda.

My blood feels like it's starting to boil.

My throat closes up.

I start to cough. The sound echoes around the large room, filling it with my contempt and disappointment.

Finally, his speech is over.

Every person on the parole board gives the prosecutor a little nod, a courtesy that neither Owen nor I got when we spoke.

By the time it's Owen's attorney's chance to speak, they are barely listening.

I can see their eyes glazing over and two of them check their phones. This is the most important moment in Owen's life and these people, who are supposed to make their decision about his freedom, can't wait to get out of here.

Once his attorney sits down, silence falls.

"Well, thank you all for coming. We will make our decision and notify you all accordingly."

"Wait, what?" I whisper under my breath. Owen glances back at me, shrugging his shoulders.

"They aren't going to decide now?" I ask his lawyer.

"No," she says. "They never do."

30

WHEN I TALK TO HIM...

Owen doesn't seem as surprised by this as I am. I reach over to him to give him a hug, but a guard blocks me.

"I am sorry, there is no touching."

Owen shrugs his shoulders. He is used to this kind of treatment, but after all of these years somehow, I still am not.

Why can't we even hold hands? They are afraid that I will pass him something illegal, but I promise that I won't. That's not enough, of course.

The incarcerated are in there for many reasons, which all boil down to one; they are liars.

They will tell anyone anything they want to hear to get what they want. At least, that's what prosecutors, guards, judges, and the parole board think.

"How long will it take them?" I ask his lawyer whose name I already forgot.

"I have no idea," she says. "It depends. Sometimes, we hear by the end of the day, sometimes it takes a week."

I shake my head. It's almost as if this whole system is designed to make prisoners and their families feel completely out of control.

Perhaps, that's the point, huh?

But Owen isn't guilty.

Technically, he was in the car while the robbery took place. Still, there's the truth that exists on paper and then there's the real truth. I'm not saying he's completely innocent. He's just not guilty the way other people in there are.

Owen's hands are shackled in the front attached by a long chain to his feet. Dressed like this, he looks like a scary person to let back out into society.

If I were sitting on that parole board

and this was the first time I saw him, I'd have a hard time saying that the world would be a safe place were he walking among us.

I watch the guard lead him away and listen to the loud clinking sound that the chain makes with each of his laborious steps.

I watch the parole board shuffle out the side entrance near the front, leaving all of the paperwork on the table in front of them.

I wonder whose case they will hear next.

"You know that he got a shitty deal," I say, turning to the prosecutor.

Up close, he doesn't look like he's even in his forties, but he already has a head full of gray hair. Hereditary or an occupational hazard?

He puts the papers in front of him into a briefcase without acknowledging me.

"You don't agree?" I ask.

"It's not up to me to say," he says, getting up.

"What do you mean?"

"Much of this case is out of my control. There are statutes that govern what sentencing he got. He refused to cooperate with the prosecutor's office, so our hands were tied."

His voice is robotic and detached. He wasn't the one who originally prosecuted the case and I wonder how much he knows about any of the details.

"Please, there must be something you can do," I plead, touching his arm.

He looks down at my hand on his suit jacket and then up at me. I pull away.

"It's not up to me," he says. "It's up to them. But for what it's worth, you made a really nice speech."

"You think it helped?" I ask.

"It didn't hurt," he says, walking past me. "Listen, I have another hearing in here in half an hour. I have to run to my car to get my sandwich."

I've always thought about lawyers living the high life.

Fancy apartments. Nice cars.

Definitely, not people who stuff their

faces with smelly bologna sandwiches on their short breaks.

"Glamorous life of a district attorney," he says, reading my mind.

He takes a gulp from a can of soda that he also brought from home. "From what I read here, your brother should've turned state's evidence when they made him the offer. That was the only way he would've avoided such a harsh sentence."

"He didn't want to snitch on his friends," I say, using his words. "I tried to convince him but he wouldn't budge."

"Well, his friends aren't exactly the easiest people to testify against, but if he had then he wouldn't have spent so much time in prison."

I narrow my eyes.

"Wait, what do you mean?"

"They are pretty connected. Organized crime," he explains. "Not exactly the type that's easy to testify against. Especially if you're from Charlestown."

This is news to me.

"Was my brother also involved?"

"Yes, of course. You didn't know?"

I shrug. "I knew that he hung around with some bad people but I didn't know that he did anything...illegal."

"He was a well-known dealer of meth and opioids," the prosecutor says. "Ran a small crew, with four guys under him. The ones he was with that night were also a bit higher up in the organization. They called each other managers. The ones who worked for them were entry level associates."

I shake my head.

"None of this is on record, of course," he continues. "But it was well known in the department. The cops never had enough to really put him away, so when he was arrested on this charge, they threw the book at him, so to speak."

It's hard to explain how it feels to find out that something is a lie after years of thinking it was the truth.

All I can say is that it tastes like bile.

I feel like Owen and I have gotten very close recently. He wrote me every day telling me everything about his life. The thing that he neglected to share was his past.

"You didn't know?" the prosecutor asks.

31

WHEN WE WAIT...

I stare at the prosecutor, hoping that I don't look too bewildered. He asks me again if I knew any of what he had just told me about Owen. Do I look like I do? I want to ask him. Instead, I just shake my head no.

"Well, pretty much everyone in prison has a past. That doesn't change the fact that he might have been rehabilitated."

This piques my interest. "You think he should be released?" I ask.

"That's not what I said."

"That's what you argued."

"It's my job to argue for the state, whether or not I agree with their position."

I shake my head, unable to fathom what it would be like to make arguments that I didn't believe in. I can hardly make arguments that I do believe in.

"What are you saying?" I ask.

"I'm saying that there are a lot of people who are serving time they probably shouldn't be. And there are a lot of people who are living the good life on the outside, who probably should be incarcerated for life. The system isn't perfect but it's all we have."

"Where does my brother fit in?" I ask.

"Somewhere in the gray area. He did something wrong. He got convicted. Should he be paying for that misdeed all of these years later?" He sighs deeply. "I'm not so sure."

I look down at my shoes not sure what else to talk to him about.

"Listen, I have to get back inside and review my notes. But it was nice talking to you, Olive, right?" He extends his hand and I realize that I don't know his name.

"Yes, Olive Kernes. And you are?" I ask.

"Bradley Bookout." He gives me a firm handshake. "It has been a pleasure."

Watching him walk back into the room, I wonder if the next argument he makes for the state he will actually believe in.

Or maybe, he has done this for so long, that he's past the point of caring.

Our legal system is based on the assumption that if both sides fight hard, then the truth will emerge.

How does that saying go about what happens when you assume? You make an *ass* out of *u* and *me*?

I texted Nicholas as soon as the hearing was over so that he could drive from the hotel. There was no point in him waiting for me in the parking lot because I had no idea when everything would come to an end.

"How long have you been waiting?" I ask, climbing into the rental car, a new model Range Rover.

"How did it go?" he asks.

He starts the engine but doesn't move the car from park. He turns his body toward mine and waits.

"It was in the administrative part of the building but I still had to go through all the checks like I was a visitor," I start. "Those can take an enormous amount of time, depending on how many guards are on duty and how many visitors show up. In the past, I had to wait in a lineup of cars at three a.m. just to get in at six. But today, because I had an appointment, they actually let me through."

This isn't really what he is eager to hear but I can't bring myself to tell him the rest. Not yet.

"Let's just get out of here," I say. "I'm starving."

WE DON'T TALK MUCH on the way to the restaurant. I'm so famished I want to ask him to pull over at the nearest fast food place so I can order everything on the menu, but I keep my cool. It's the anxiety talking.

Besides, I've made a promise to myself

to eat clean and healthy for thirty days. No processed food. No sugar. No bread.

I haven't eaten meat in years and, for this challenge, I quit dairy as well.

What's left? Greens like asparagus and celery and kale. Fish - salmon and tilapia are my favorites, and eggs.

I've been cooking with olive oil instead of butter for a while now and have taught myself to snack on sunflower seeds and walnuts in moderation.

This morning I broke the rules and had a power bar. But this evening, I'm going to stick to them.

I scan the menu and quickly order sautéed salmon with asparagus and green beans on the side. Technically, green beans are also not allowed, beans are a processed food, but the cheating here isn't out of control. It's when Nicholas suggests a dessert of chocolate cheesecake that my mouth really starts to water.

Chocolate has always been my downfall. A few years ago, I switched to very dark chocolate like eighty-five or ninety percent instead of milk because those bars have a lot less sugar in them. I developed my palate and now I can throw back one or two of them on a bad day, quite easily. I love the bitterness and the tartness as well as the complexity in the taste.

"You've been quiet all evening," Nicholas says, as I stare at his gigantic plate of pasta, yearning for just one bite.

"Just thinking about your food. It looks delicious."

"It is," he says, taking a bite. "You want some?"

"Yes, but no."

"It's okay if you have some."

No, it's not. I have made a commitment and this time I'm going to stick to it. I have started and stopped this thirty-day challenge about five times already, always giving up just a day into it. Beans and a power bar are not such bad cheats, but if I take even one bite of pasta, I know that I won't be able to stop.

"You look beautiful just the way you are," Nicholas says.

"Thank you, I appreciate it." I give him a nod.

I'm glad that he finds me attractive but it's not really him who I'm doing this for. I appreciate and love my body but at the same time I know I need a change.

I want to get out of this spiral where whenever anything bad happens, I immediately turn to food to make it better.

Today is a hard day to say no, but if I can stay strong today then I can do it on all of those other days as well.

"So, are you ever going to tell me what happened?" Nicholas asks.

32

WHEN WE EAT...

Back in Hawaii, Nicholas didn't want to let me come back here. We had a fight about it. I did something that was probably stupid and too dangerous. The only reason I'm here at all is that he chartered a private plane and traveled with me.

I look into Nicholas' eyes. Under the candlelight, the flecks of green are almost gold. Owen's warnings echo in my head.

Can I really trust him? I don't know much about him.

But then again, I don't know much about Owen either.

"The prosecutor told me that he was a lot more involved in the gang than I knew," I finally say.

Owen's going to be my metaphor. I don't know what Nicholas is hiding from me but I want him to know that I don't appreciate it.

"I'm sorry about that," he says nonchalantly.

"He lied to me. All of these years. It doesn't feel good," I say.

"Well, maybe he had a good reason."

I clench my jaw. "Like what?"

"Isn't every conversation you had recorded? Don't they check all the mail and the emails?"

I nod.

"Well, there you go. He didn't want to implicate himself in anything by telling you the truth."

That is such a convenient explanation. It's almost too convenient.

I've played enough games for one day. I've heard enough untruths.

"You wouldn't lie to me, would you?" I ask.

"It depends," he says without missing a beat.

"On what?"

"On what it was about. You already know that you do not know much about my business."

"But I will in the future?" I insist.

"No, I can't say that you will. Some things you just can't know. It will be too dangerous."

I lean over the table. "You know, I'm a big girl. I'm getting really sick of all of these men in my life trying to decide what I should and shouldn't know."

Nicholas sits back, completely unfazed.

"I'm sorry you feel that way but it's not going to change," he says. "There are certain parts about my life that you just cannot know about."

"Like what?" I challenge him. He narrows his eyes and gives me a wink.

"Like what's on that laptop you got for me," he says.

"That's the first and last job that I'm doing for you without knowing everything."

The smirk vanishes suddenly. Nicholas leans forward over his plate. "That's not up to you. You agreed to do as I say, whatever I need you to do. If you don't comply, if you demand answers that I can't provide out of fear for your safety, then I rescind my offer."

Each word of his statement lands like a punch. I didn't want to get into this now. My day has been too emotional as it is.

He sees the disappointment on my face. "I am sorry. I don't mean to be so harsh in my language, but I just want to be very clear about what is going to happen," Nicholas adds.

The only thing that I am clear about is that I am tired of all of the lies.

I have spent the day listening to Owen lie on the stand.

For years, I believed that he was wrongfully convicted, or at the very least, doing way too much time for the crime that he had committed.

But today, I found out that he was actually a criminal for a long time, one that eluded the police. That's probably why he refused to testify against his friends. Not out of some perverse sense of loyalty but rather out of obligation. Who knows what they had on him that they could use as retribution?

And now...sitting here across the table from Nicholas, the man who stirs the kind of emotions within me that I have never felt before, I am being forced to accept more lies from him.

Only this time, he is warning me about them.

He will hide things.

He will lie to me.

He will obfuscate the truth.

I just have to accept it because that's part of our agreement.

Well, fuck that!

"No, absolutely not," I say.

Nicholas rubs one of his temples with his index finger. "What are you talking about?"

"That's not our agreement and if that's what you want to make it now, then I am not going along with it."

"You can't," he says.

"Yes, I can. I'm back home. Just get on your plane and get the hell out of here. I don't need you."

The waiter comes over to our table and we both sit up straight and force polite smiles. This a nice restaurant with a water view and no entrees under twenty bucks.

"Let's calm down," Nicholas says after the waiter leaves.

"I am calm." I look straight into his eyes without flinching one bit. "I am just done with listening to lies."

He takes a deep breath. He looks away first.

"I don't mean to lie to you. There is just certain information that I am not privy to discuss."

"What does that mean?"

HIs eyes widen as if he is surprised by my question. I tilt my head to one side and wait for him to explain. But he doesn't.

"What do you do for a living?" I ask. Again, he doesn't reply. "It's a simple question. Some people are lawyers. Doctors. Firemen."

"I am none of those things."

"So, what is it that *you* do?" I have no idea where all of this pent up energy and anger is coming from but it's just rushing to the surface and out of my mouth.

"You know what I do, Olive," Nicholas says quietly.

I have some idea, of course. I know that he's a thief and a con man. What I don't know is who he works for and the extent of what it is that he does.

"I think you need some rest. Today was a very emotional day for you," he says, putting his hand on mine. I jerk it away.

"Don't tell me what I need," I say. "I know what I need. The truth."

Somewhere in the back of my mind I know that he is right. The reason I'm so emotional is because of everything that happened at Owen's hearing and the fact that I still don't know what the resolution was.

But I can't admit that to him. Not now.

My pride won't let me.

"You want to know something true?" he asks, cocking his head.

I nod.

"That woman who surprised you at Dallas's hotel room..." his voice trails off.

"What happened?" I ask.

"She's dead," Nicholas says.

33

WHEN I FIND OUT THE TRUTH...

His words reverberate in my head over and over again but I still don't understand. How could she be dead?

"Rosemary?" I ask.

"You know her name?" Nicholas hisses. "How do you know her name?"

I shrug. "She introduced herself when she came in."

"Okay, tell me everything that happened."

I run through the story that I told him earlier. Only this time, my mind doesn't immediately go to my lust for Dallas or the jealousy that I wanted Nicholas to feel. I keep my voice low and speak in metaphors because I don't want anyone around us to hear.

When the waiter comes back and asks us about dessert, I refuse to see the menu to not even give myself the chance to be tempted by something dark and delicious. Nicholas asks for the check and hands him his card without even looking at it. Neither of us says anything while we wait for it to come back for him to sign. Once he does, we promptly exit the restaurant.

In the privacy of his rental car, Nicholas wants me to go over everything that happened that night with Dallas yet again.

"Do not neglect to mention a single detail," he insists.

I take a deep breath and start at the beginning. Once I describe how I felt the first time I saw Dallas, Nicholas' face contorts for a moment and then relaxes. He clenches his jaw.

"You found him attractive?" he asks, stroking his Adam's apple. I nod.

"Why?"

"I don't know. He was hot. WE had this...chemistry."

He smooths down the cuffs of his shirt and then looks at me again.

"Why is this important?" I ask. "I mean, why do you even care? Tell me what happened to Rosemary."

"Rosemary's real name was Caitlyn Montgomery Sudik," he says without missing a beat. "She grew up in Florida and trained at the Bloom Academy."

Is that a school? I'm not sure why this is relevant. I give him a blank stare.

"The Bloom Academy is a secret and very elite private school that teaches men and women about the art of seduction," Nicholas explains. "She was recruited and taught well and has since traveled the world and made a lot of money for the organization."

"What organization?" I whisper.

He shakes his head. He is telling me a lot more than he did before so I don't push for now.

"So, what happened to her?" I ask.

"She never came back after meeting with Dallas. She texted her boyfriend that she was meeting up with a friend of hers but they never met and her friend didn't know a thing about this supposed meeting. Her body was found yesterday, deep in the rainforest by a couple of hikers. The police are clueless but my sources suspect that it's Dallas's doing."

I put my hand over my mouth.

If the police don't know who did it, what sources does Nicholas have that tell him that it was Dallas?

"You were the last person to see her alive," Nicholas says as if he can read my mind. "Well, not the last, but you were the one who left them in that room together. Alive and well."

"Are you saying that this is my fault?" I ask.

"No, not at all. It's mine."

"How is it your fault?"

"I should have never told you about that laptop or that job," he says. "I'm just glad that it wasn't you."

I hope that whatever was on that laptop was worth it, I want to say. But I immediately catch myself.

What could that laptop possibly

contain that would be worth a human life? A young, healthy life of an innocent at that?

"Do you really think Dallas did it?" I whisper.

Nicholas gives me one conclusive nod.

I shake my head, no, no, no.

"What do you think happened?" I ask.

"He might have seen that the laptop was switched and thought that she was in on it. Or he might have found it suspicious that you just suddenly left and again took it out on her."

I look down and rub the outside of my knuckles on my left hand.

"I'm not saying this was your fault, not at all."

"You don't have to."

"But I am involved in some serious shit, Olive. With some serious people. And the less you know about it the better."

My stomach begins to roil.

Doesn't he realize that this whole thing happened because I didn't know *enough*?

He should've told me that I was going there.

He should've trusted me enough to let me handle it.

If we had followed his original plan, Rosemary would still be alive.

"Dallas Stone is a savage. He has killed many people. I only know of a few, but that's enough. That's why I didn't want you doing that. Not for me. Not for any offer."

Owen thinks you killed a few people as well, and yet here we are, I want to say. But I bite my tongue.

Growing weary of second-guessing and going over every regret from that night, I pivot our conversation.

"How long have you been tracking him?" I ask.

"For about a year. That's why I set up my headquarters in Maui. I knew that he was going to be there to go to one of those parties, just not when."

"I'm so sorry," I say.

"For what?" he says. "That your friend and my friend are frisky and decided to go to a sex club together? You didn't know what they did together. And neither did I."

I nod. We sit in silence for a while staring into the distance.

My thoughts return to Rosemary.

She was so beautiful and perfect and now she's dead.

It's all because of me.

Dallas might have done it but were it not for me, she would still be drawing breath.

I glance over at Nicholas. His mind is likewise occupied.

Rain starts to fall and we both watch the droplets smash into the windshield.

How did everything get so complicated? I wonder.

34

WHEN WE KISS...

Nicholas booked a few nights at the Ritz, but I don't feel like staying at a five-star hotel. Instead, I invite him over to my place.

We have the lease for six more months and I have no idea if we should give it up. Frankly, the world has been spinning so fast recently that it's hard to find solid footing.

After giving Nicholas a brief tour around the living room, the kitchen, and my bedroom, I glance down at my phone and realize that I hadn't texted Sydney back since this morning. She even left me a few voice mail messages, and she never leaves voice mails.

Scanning the transcriptions instead of listening to her frantic voice, I know that I can't *not* write her back. I need to put her mind at ease even though all I want to do is to curl up in my sheets and not come out of bed for days.

"Make yourself at home," I say, standing in the middle of the kitchen.

I quickly type up a long paragraph summarizing everything that happened and press send. I add another text for good measure: *can't text anymore tonight. Will message you tomorrow for sure.*

Instead of long paragraphs, Sydney has always been a rapid fire type of replier. Every thought gets its individual line.

OMG, seriously?

I was thinking about you all day.

Btw, James is amazing!!!

Okay, let's talk tomorrow.

How's our apt?

.   .   .

I READ them quickly but want to not write back but I can't stop myself.

Everything's great here. Still have to figure out what to do about the lease. R u moving to HI?

MAYBE?? Yes! No! I don't know.
Shrug emoji.

NICHOLAS PARKS himself on the couch and buries his head in his phone. After I put mine down, I see him swiping through emails and checking different apps for who knows what.

"So, what now?" I ask.

He mumbles something without looking up.

"What's going to happen now?" I ask again.

He finishes typing something and looks up. "What are you referring to?"

"I mean, we came here for the hearing. I really appreciate you letting me do that."

I cringe at my use of the word *let*. He didn't let me. I don't need his permission.

Yet, I still want to thank him for what he did: bringing me here on his private plane in all of the comforts that kind of lifestyle affords.

"Thank you for not rescinding the offer," I say. "I still want to do it."

"One year with me? You sure you can handle that?" he jokes.

"It's you that you should worry about." I smile. His hand grazes his temple just as he drops his chin.

"Yeah, I'm getting that sense."

Our eyes lock on each other's and we share a moment. Suddenly, nothing else exists except the two of us. I don't know much about him and he doesn't know much about me but that's part of the attraction. It's the mystery that gives me all of the feels.

I take a step toward him, he takes two closer to me.

He brings his hands to my face. They smell like lemon.

He squeezed one into his drink over dinner.

The scent is intoxicating. I stand up on my tiptoes and press my lips to his.

I bury my fingers in his hair. It is so soft and luxurious I can lose myself in it.

He opens his mouth and our tongues intertwine. But only for a moment. Then he starts kissing my neck.

Warmth starts to radiate from somewhere in between my legs and course through the rest of my body.

My hands search for an entrance into his flesh. I peel off his jacket, dropping it to the floor.

His shirt is tucked in. Tightly. His mouth returns to mine as I tug on it trying to keep our lips together. I laugh. Then he laughs. He pulls the shirt up from the back and helps me unbutton the front.

I do one button for his two.

Once the shirt is shed, I take a second to admire the body underneath. I run my fingers down his washboard abs. Then I run them back up again. I kiss his nipples, one at a time.

He takes off my cardigan and kisses my arms, from the shoulders down to the crook of my elbows. Instead of letting him, I wrap my arms around his neck. He tries to unbutton my blouse, but I don't even let him untuck it. Instead, I just pull up my skirt over my butt and place his palms on my cheeks.

"Hmmm," he moans, squeezing them gently.

"In case there's any confusion," I say slowly. "This is me begging you to do it."

He pulls away from me. His eyes light up. Even twinkle. I roll mine.

"Oh, is that right?" He squeezes me tightly.

"Please, fuck me," I whisper into his ear.

"Yes, ma'am," he says, spinning me around.

There's a perfectly good bed right over there.

My roommate is six thousand miles away.

We have all night to enjoy ourselves and our bodies.

But I don't want any of that right now.

I have been teased enough by this man. I want him to take me from behind. I want him to fuck me. I want him to do it so hard that I see stars.

Nicholas' hands grasp onto my thighs and fold me over the kitchen island. It's the perfect height for this exact activity.

I grab on tightly to the edge, bracing myself for impact. But then I remember that I'm still wearing underwear.

It's not really much, just a black thong that can easily be slid to the side.

Instead of doing that, he tugs at it slightly and watches it fall down to the floor. By the time, I step out of it and press his body to mine, I realize that it wasn't just my thong that he had removed. We are now flesh to flesh. I can feel his hard dick against me.

I spread my legs. I lean over. I wait.

"Get the fuck off her," a stranger's low deep voice says.

35

WHEN THERE IS AN INTERRUPTION...

For a second, I think that the voice might belong to Nicholas. But it's raspier, older than his. When I turn back, I see a man in all black. Black long sleeve shirt, black pants, black combat boots, black gloves, and a black ski mask.

He's pointing a gun with a long barrel right at Nicholas' head. My throat closes up. Nicholas takes a step away from me.

On instinct, I pull down my skirt but Nicholas doesn't make a move to get dressed. His pants are still at his ankles and he just stands there, motionless. His shoulders spread wide, his arms at his sides.

It takes significant effort to pull my eyes away from the weapon. But after a moment, I focus on him instead. The guy with his finger on the trigger.

Who are you? I wonder.

I can't make out a single distinguishing characteristic except for his height, which is way over six feet. I don't even know what race he is because the slits in the mask are too small to distinguish the skin color.

"What do you want?" Nicholas says.

"The girl is coming with me."

"No," Nicholas says, but then the perpetrator points the gun at him.

"I'm not here to kill anyone, but I'm ready to do it," he says. "Don't get in my way."

My head is spinning. He's here for me? Why? Who is he? What does he want with *me*?

"You mind if I pull up my pants?" Nicholas says.

His voice sounds strange. Casual somehow.

Sing- songy even.

The usual intensity is gone.

But why? Maybe to appear calmer or not so threatening. Though why would *he* seem threatening?

The guy shakes his head no.

"C'mon, man," Nicholas whines. He actually elongates the a in man so that it resembles a sound that a sheep would make.

The man grabs me by my arm and pulls me toward him.

I look back at Nicholas. My eyes open wide. His hands are strong and powerful and they pinch at my neck. I try to resist but he keeps waving his gun over my head.

The gun goes off piercing my ear drum.

When my head stops pounding long enough for me to open my eyes, I see the guy lying on his back with a little black dot in between his eyes.

"Are you okay?" Nicholas says, throwing his arms around me.

Tears stream down my face making it impossible for me to speak.

He holds me for a few minutes and lets me cry on his shoulder. I feel safe in his arms, even though I had just watched him execute a man in front of me.

"Should I call the police?" I ask, keeping my eyes closed. Nicholas pulls away abruptly.

"Absolutely not."

I reach out for him again, but he just walks away.

"Not now," he says curtly.

Nicholas picks up his phone. Okay, he wants to make the call to the cops. That makes sense.

I don't even know how to begin to explain what just happened.

"Yes, I'm calling for Katherine Hepburn. Urgency level 9," he says and hangs up.

Katherine Hepburn, the dead movie star? Is that someone's name? Why did he call her instead of the cops?

He walks over to the sink and opens the lower cupboard.

"Do you have any...?" he asks, turning around all of the bottles and searching through the mess of crap underneath there.

Before I can answer him, he pulls out a

pair of Sydney's canary yellow cleaning gloves.

"Why do you need those?" I ask.

My blood runs cold. He needs them to hide evidence.

"But you did nothing wrong," I plead.

My voice gets really high and uneven, even cracking, as a result of my disappointment. "He burst in here and pointed his gun at us. He was going to kidnap me. I'm sure that the police will understand."

As I talk, Nicholas continues to work.

He pats down the body and checks his pockets.

What is he looking for?

"No identification," Nicholas says. "He's a professional."

"Professional what?" I gasp.

"Killer."

The word ping-pongs around my head like an echo.

Professional killer. What did a professional killer want with me? I don't know anything. I haven't done anything.

Why would someone even bother to hire someone like this?

Nicholas grabs a bottle of bleach from under the sink and puts it on the counter. There isn't much blood.

Actually, there's hardly any at all. I should probably offer to help him clean up, but I can't make a single muscle in my body budge.

The buzzer goes off. I nearly jump up in place.

My heart starts to race.

I get drenched in sweat, and I start to shiver at the same time.

"Don't worry," Nicholas says. "It's Katherine Hepburn."

When he opens the door, a well put together woman in her fifties comes in. She has an expensive haircut and she smells of Chanel No. 5 perfume. Dressed like a lawyer on television, she carries a large leather purse on her shoulder. She doesn't look anything like the movie star, yet she somehow gives off a similar vibe.

Nicholas is about to close the door behind her, but then two men appear.

Outfitted in hoodies with the word, Daly Moving Company, and back support belts with suspenders on top, they are carrying flat boxes as well as large bags big enough to fit a huge living room rug. Or a body.

36

WHEN THEY TAKE CARE OF
THE PROBLEM...

My breathing slows down along with my heartbeat. A little bit of fear dissipates with each exhalation.

Without saying a word, the movers just get to work. Katherine Hepburn gives them instructions and they do as they are told.

First, they unzip the rug bag and lay it flat on the floor. It's black canvas on the outside and plastic on the side. Very convenient in case there's bleeding. The bag looks expensive, exactly the type of bag that this type of woman would have.

They place the body inside the bag and zip it closed. I am surprised by how little blood there is on the floor.

The woman motions to Nicholas and he kneels down and soaks up the blood with the paper towels. Afterward, he pours bleach on the spot and rubs until all of the visible residue is gone.

Katherine Hepburn opens her bag without taking it off her shoulder and pulls out a small device. Someone kills the lights. She sprays something onto the floor. The device emits a cool blue light.

"Is it not out?" I ask him.

"The Luminol is reacting with the bleach right there," Nicholas says. "That's why it's all bright like that."

Katherine Hepburn takes slow careful steps away from where the body was lying.

"What is she doing?" I ask.

"Checking for hidden blood splatter," he explains.

Nicholas, the movers, and I wait while she carefully makes her way around the perimeter, spraying and illuminating as she sees fit.

Once she is satisfied that there are no particles of blood anywhere else in the apartment, she turns on her heels and tells the movers to get started.

Her voice is low, quiet, and authoritative.

The movers take the boxes that they brought with them and fold them up. They tape the bottom and the top but don't put anything inside.

They make a total of four of them. Even though the boxes are empty, there is visible strain on their faces once they lift them. Katherine Hepburn opens the door for them and they disappear down the hallway.

"What are they doing?" I ask.

"You are moving some of your stuff to storage," Nicholas says. "You hired the Daly company to help you. You are also selling this rug here to a buyer from a rug clearinghouse in New York. You don't know her name but you found her through her advertisement in the Boston Magazine."

I nod. The story comes out of his mouth so naturally I almost believe it even though I know the truth.

Katherine Hepburn pulls out a copy of

the magazine and places it on my coffee table.

"Is your ad really in there?" I ask.

"Of course," she says.

Taking out a large plastic Ziplock bag from her purse, she opens it for Nicholas who places all of the blood-soaked paper towels into it.

He sprays some bleach on the spot where they were laying, wipes it with another sheet, and places that into her bag as well.

Everything about this operation is so professional and efficient that it makes my head spin. I pick up the magazine and go to the back where most of the ads are.

"Page one thirty-five," Katherine Hepburn says.

The movers come back.

Arguing about the Patriots, they leave the front door wide open and grab the black bag, one on each side.

"Shit, this rug is no joke," one of them says.

They let the door slam behind them.

I flip to the page that she told me and

there at the bottom I see that someone had circled Prestige Rug Company's advertisement in thin blue ink.

"Thank you very much, ma'am," Katherine Hepburn says, handing me a check for $700 made out in my name. Prestige Rug Company's name and address are prominently displayed at the top. It's signed by K. C. Prestige. "It was a pleasure doing business with you."

"Thank you," I mumble. "You, too."

She walks out of the door, just at the movers come back for their last load.

"We'll drive this right over to the storage unit," one of them says. "Thanks again."

They let the door slam again and then Nicholas and I are alone.

Their smiles and their acting are so convincing that I have to look around for a second and remind myself of what really happened.

Or maybe I shouldn't.

Maybe it's better to just pretend and improvise a different outcome just like they are.

"Well, that was...efficient," I say slowly, not entirely sure if that's the right word for it.

"I need a drink. You want one?" Nicholas asks.

"Oh, God, yes!"

Nicholas pours us both generous amounts of whiskey and we sit down on the couch.

The amber colored liquid ignites my taste buds with a pleasing combination of leather, cedar wood, and candied almonds.

It burns my throat as it slides down and leaves a bit of an orange pith aftertaste.

"Why didn't you want to call the police?" I ask even though I suspect that I already know the answer.

"Olive, I have to tell you something," Nicholas says.

37

WHEN I FIND OUT WHY...

I nod. I don't need to brace myself for impact. I already know what he's about to say.

That guy, the professional killer, wasn't really after me. He may have wanted to kidnap me but this whole thing has to do with Nicholas and the kind of business that he's in.

"Someone is after you," he says. "I killed this one but they aren't going to stop."

I turn to face him. His words don't make any sense.

"What are you talking about?" I ask when he doesn't elaborate.

"I was foolish enough to think that I

could protect you," he says without turning toward me.

"Remember when I told you that Ashley asked me to watch out for you?" he asks. I nod. "There's a contract out on your head."

I sit back into the couch. I press the nails of my hand into the palms of my other until they leave creases.

"The reason why Owen got a parole hearing is that he provided testimony against someone over something that happened in prison. I don't know the details but that's why the district attorney arranged for his hearing."

"What does that mean?"

"It means that the people he testified against are out for blood. He doesn't have a wife or children, you are the closest living member of his family. He loves you and they want him to hurt."

"How do you know this?" I ask, shaking my head in disbelief.

"I'm a pretty well connected guy, Olive. I have feelers set up on the streets. They tell me what they hear."

"And what is that?"

"These guys want to make him pay."

No, something doesn't make sense. Owen loves me. He would never set me up like this. He's not our mother. He would never betray me.

"He doesn't know about this," Nicholas says. "If that's what you are thinking. He thinks that his life is in danger in prison but I doubt that he knows that they would go so low as to try to kidnap and kill his sister."

That makes me feel good but only momentarily.

"That's why I didn't want you to come back to Boston," Nicholas continues. "I know that you must've thought that I was some sort of possessive asshole, but I didn't want to tell you this and I didn't know how else to protect you."

My mind quickly reviews the highlights of everything that has happened ever since I met him.

"So, this whole time, this offer you made me...I thought you needed me to be your partner. I thought that's why you were paying me." My words rush out all at once, in fragments, barely making any sense.

"I couldn't very well kidnap you against your will," Nicholas says. "But I needed to protect you."

"For Ashley?" I ask.

"At first, but then...for me."

"For you?" I ask. I feel an invisible feather tickle the back of my throat and cough.

"Yeah, I kinda grew to like you," Nicholas says, giving me a little kick with his foot. The flecks of gold in his eyes light up.

"So, what now?" I ask.

"I don't know but we need to be very careful. These men that he testified against have very powerful friends. That guy I killed, he is one of the best assassins out there. The only reason I got the upper hand was that he got distracted."

"What exactly happened?"

"It's always difficult when you have two people to keep the gun on, especially if you're not exactly willing to kill immediately," Nicholas explains. "He wanted to take you somewhere. Probably to his boss who would use you as leverage to get Owen to do something."

"To take back his confession?" I ask.

"Maybe." He shrugs. "Or something else entirely. I have no idea. The problem was that he didn't want to kill me. He didn't know I would be here and he definitely didn't know who I was. That's why I was acting so aloof."

I nod my head, processing everything that he's saying.

"When I saw him look at you, I grabbed his gun out of his hand and shot him."

"Just like that?" I ask.

"You wanted me to talk to him first?" He laughs.

I run my fingers around the rim of my empty glass. The whiskey makes me feel warm and cozy, slowing down my thoughts to something less than the speed of sound.

My phone rings. I look at the screen. It's a private number. I'm tempted to make it go to voicemail, but at the very last moment I don't.

As soon as I hear the robotic voice on

the other end and wait for it to make the connection, I know that it's Owen.

"Guess what?" he says. He is so excited he can barely contain himself. "They granted my parole."

I'm stunned. My tongue touches the roof of my mouth. He says my name over and over again before I can bring myself to respond.

"Are you okay?"

"I'm fine," I lie. "I'm just really happy for you."

Nicholas furrows his brow, confused. I hold out my palm to tell him to wait.

"Is this normal for them to grant parole so quickly?" I ask.

Nicholas nods, understanding immediately what I'm talking about.

"I don't know, but who cares, I got it!" Owen says. He takes a beat. "You don't seem very excited."

"No, no, it's not that," I say quickly. "I am very excited."

I shift my weight from one side to another and cross and uncross my arms. Nicholas puts his arms around me. Having his body so close to mine calms me down a bit.

"So, what happens now?" I raise my voice, forcing the excitement.

"They told me that they will be releasing me tomorrow. Actually tonight. They always do it in the middle of the night, starting the process around one a.m."

"Why is that?" I ask.

"There are a bunch of steps," Owen says. "They take me to a series of waiting rooms. There is a lot to process. The stuff that I collected in prison. Books, writings, things like that. And then they have to return the belongings that I brought here as well."

I nod along pretending that any of this makes sense.

"Okay, don't take this the wrong way," I say. "But isn't it a little bit suspicious that you're getting released so...soon?"

There's a long pause. "What exactly are you saying?"

I shake my head. "Did you....do something to make this happen?"

I know that this is the wrong thing to

ask just as the words come out of my
mouth.

"What the *fuck* are you saying, Olive?"
Owen demands to know. The tone of his
voice shifts from loving brother to
convicted felon.

"Nothing. I'm not saying anything."

"What the *fuck* are you *implying* then?"

Owen's education has come a long way
since he first went in. When he started
doing time, he was an angry young man
who couldn't formulate a coherent
sentence about his feelings or anything that
was happening to him.

But when he learned to read and write
and then spent years educating himself in
his cell and the prison library, he developed
words for his thoughts and feelings.

He was no longer the irate toddler who
knew what he wanted but couldn't quite
express it.

"I am just surprised by how this whole
thing has unfolded, that's all," I play dumb.

I want to ask him who he ratted on, but
this isn't the right time or place. Everything
we are saying is being recorded. He knows

it as well as I do. Besides, as soon as he is out, he will have plenty of time to explain himself.

"You're not the only one," Owen says. "But it has happened to a few of my friends. There's a major overcrowding problem so they're letting out some non-violent, well-behaving inmates on parole earlier than they probably would have otherwise. The new governor has done a lot to make it happen."

"That's great," I say under my breath.

Oh, hmmm. Maybe this is it then. Nothing suspicious. Maybe the guy who broke into my apartment had *nothing* to do with Owen. I was so quick to judge him and to put the blame on him. Nicholas' explanation seemed so plausible, but what if I was wrong? What if that guy had something to do with Nicholas instead?

A robot voice comes on the line and tells us that we only have a minute left.

"Will you be here to pick me up?" Owen asks.

"When? Where?"

"At the front gate of the prison. Six

a.m.," he says. "Be there at six but it may take longer. Sometimes there's a delay and it's out of my control."

"Yes, of course, I'll wait," I say. "After all of these years I'm pretty used to working around their schedule."

Owen sighs and then chokes up. When he gathers his composure, he says, "*We* won't have to work on anyone's schedule after tomorrow."

"No, we won't." I smile.

When I'm about to say goodbye, Owen interrupts me.

"You have no idea how much it means that you were there for me all of these years. I know that we were never very close as kids, but you taking the time to write me all the time and talk to me...it really made the time bearable. I love you, Olive."

"I love you, too," I say, tears welling up in my eyes.

I hang up the phone and stare at the blank screen, wiping a rogue tear from my eye.

"He's getting out," I say. "He's really getting out."

Nicholas doesn't reply. Standing up, he paces in front of me in a circular motion. His nostrils flare. His chest thrusts out with his elbows firmly planted away from his body.

"Are you...upset?" I ask.

He cracks his knuckles. Glaring at me, his eyes tighten and then turn to ice.

"You can't go there," he finally says. "You can't meet him when he gets out. Absolutely not."

***

Thank you for reading TELL ME TO GO!

I hope you enjoyed continuing Nicholas and Olive's story. Can't wait to find out what happens next?

One-click TELL ME TO STAY Now!

DECADENT and delicious 3rd book of the new and addictive Tell Me series by bestselling author Charlotte Byrd.

I am not a liar or a thief or a criminal. At least, not anymore. But here I am doing things that I promised myself I would never do again.

Nicholas Crawford made me an offer I couldn't refuse. He is dangerous and damaged but so am I. Our relationship is an addiction that we have to feed.

Now, things are about to get even more complicated.

Allegiances will be tested. Lies will be told. Truths will be revealed.

We have both made promises that we

can't keep. The secrets we have uncovered only scratch the surface, and I'm afraid to find out what lies below.

All is not what it seems but I have to figure out the truth before it's too late.

One-click TELL ME TO STAY Now!

SIGN up for my **newsletter** to find out when I have new books!

You can also join my Facebook group, **Charlotte Byrd's Reader Club**, for exclusive giveaways and sneak peaks of future books.

I appreciate you sharing my books and telling your friends about them. Reviews help readers find my books! Please leave a review on your favorite site.

"BEST AUTHOR YET! Charlotte has done it again! There is a reason she is an amazing author and she continues to prove it! I was definitely not disappointed in this series!!"
★★★★★

"LOVE!!! I loved this book and the whole series!!! I just wish it didn't have to end. I am definitely a fan for life!!! ★★★★★

"Extremely captivating, sexy, steamy, intriguing, and intense!" ★★★★★

"Addictive and impossible to put down."
★★★★★

"What a magnificent story from the 1st book through book 6 it never slowed down always surprising the reader in one way or the other. Nicholas and Olive's paths crossed in a most unorthodox way and that's how their story begins it's exhilarating with that nail biting suspense that keeps you riding on the edge the whole series. You'll love it!" ★★★★★

"What is Love Worth. This is a great epic ending to this series. Nicholas and Olive have a deep connection and the mystery surrounding the deaths of the people he is accused of murdering is to be read. Olive is one strong woman with deep convictions. The twists, angst, confusion is all put together to make this worthwhile read." ★★★★★

"Fast-paced romantic suspense filled with twists and turns, danger, betrayal, and so much more." ★★★★★

"Decadent, delicious, & dangerously addictive!" - Amazon Review ★★★★★

"Titillation so masterfully woven, no reader can resist its pull. A MUST-BUY!" - Bobbi Koe, Amazon Review ★★★★★

"Captivating!" - Crystal Jones, Amazon Review ★★★★★

"Sexy, secretive, pulsating chemistry..." - Mrs. K, Amazon Reviewer ★★★★★

"Charlotte Byrd is a brilliant writer. I've read loads and I've laughed and cried. She writes a balanced book with brilliant characters. Well done!" -Amazon Review ★★★★★

"Hot, steamy, and a great storyline." - Christine Reese ★★★★★

"My oh my....Charlotte has made me a fan for life." - JJ, Amazon Reviewer ★★★★★

"Wow. Just wow. Charlotte Byrd leaves me speechless and humble... It definitely kept me on the edge of my seat. Once you pick it up, you won't put it down." - Amazon Review ★★★★★

" Intrigue, lust, and great characters...what more could you ask for?!" - Dragonfly Lady

WANT TO BE THE FIRST TO KNOW ABOUT MY UPCOMING SALES, NEW RELEASES AND EXCLUSIVE GIVEAWAYS?

Sign up for my newsletter: https://www. subscribepage.com/byrdVIPList

Join my Facebook Group: https://www. facebook.com/groups/276340079439433/

Bonus Points: Follow me on BookBub and Goodreads!

ABOUT CHARLOTTE BYRD

Charlotte Byrd is the bestselling author of romantic suspense novels. She has sold over 1 Million books and has been translated into five languages.

She lives near Palm Springs, California with her husband, son, a toy Australian Shepherd and a Ragdoll cat. Charlotte is addicted to books and Netflix and she loves hot weather and crystal blue water.

Write her here:

charlotte@charlotte-byrd.com

Check out her books here:

www.charlotte-byrd.com

Connect with her here:

www.facebook.com/charlottebyrdbooks

www.instagram.com/charlottebyrdbooks

www.twitter.com/byrdauthor

Sign up for my newsletter: https://www.subscribepage.com/byrdVIPList

Join my Facebook Group: https://www.facebook.com/groups/276340079439433/

Bonus Points: Follow me on BookBub and Goodreads!

facebook.com/charlottebyrdbooks

twitter.com/byrdauthor

instagram.com/charlottebyrdbooks

bookbub.com/profile/charlotte-byrd

ALSO BY CHARLOTTE BYRD

All books are available at ALL major retailers! If you can't find it, please email me at charlotte@charlotte-byrd.com

The Perfect Stranger Series
The Perfect Stranger
The Perfect Cover
The Perfect Lie
The Perfect Life
The Perfect Getaway

All the Lies Series
All the Lies
All the Secrets
All the Doubts

Tell me Series

Tell Me to Stop

Tell Me to Go

Tell Me to Stay

Tell Me to Run

Tell Me to Fight

Tell Me to Lie

Wedlocked Trilogy

Dangerous Engagement

Lethal Wedding

Fatal Wedding

Tangled Series

Tangled up in Ice

Tangled up in Pain

Tangled up in Lace

Tangled up in Hate

Tangled up in Love

Black Series

Black Edge

Black Rules

Black Bounds

Black Contract

Black Limit

Not into you Duet
Not into you
Still not into you

Lavish Trilogy
Lavish Lies
Lavish Betrayal
Lavish Obsession

Standalone Novels
Dressing Mr. Dalton
Debt
Offer
Unknown

Made in the USA
Monee, IL
17 April 2024

57108911R00187